Enid Blyton's

STORYTIME BOOK

Enid Blyton's
STORYTIME
BOOK

PRINTED IN DEAN & 41/43 Ludgate Hill SON Ltd. GREAT BRITAIN LONDON EC4

Printed in Great Britain by Purnell & Sons, Ltd.
Paulton (Somerset) and London

CONTENTS

The Magic Treacle-Jug

Now once when Miggle the goblin was walking home at night through Goblin Village he saw a light in Mother Tick-Tock's cottage window. He stopped and thought for a moment.

"I think I'll go and peep in," he said to himself. "Mother Tick-Tock's grandfather was a wizard, and it's said that she knows plenty of useful spells. I might see something interesting if I go and peep."

So he crept into the front garden and peeped in at the lighted window. Mother Tick-Tock was there, cutting large slices of bread, one after the other.

"I suppose those are for her children's supper," thought Miggle, counting them. "One, two, three, four, five, six, seven—yes, they are. Goodness me —does she give them just dry bread for their suppers, poor things?"

He watched carefully. He saw Mother Tick-Tock take up a small purple jug and he heard her speak to it.

"Pour me treacle,
    strong and sweet,
For a Very Special
    Treat!"

And, to Miggle's surprise, the jug left Mother Tick-Tock's hand, poised itself above a slice of bread, and poured out good, thick,

7

yellow treacle! Then it balanced itself above the next slice
and poured more treacle. Then it went to the third slice.

"Good gracious me! How can a little jug like that hold so
much treacle!" thought Miggle, in surprise. "Look at it,
pouring thickly over one slice after another. What lovely
treacle too—oooh, I wish I had some of it!"

Mother Tick-Tock suddenly caught sight of Miggle's face
at the window, and, leaving the jug pouring treacle on the last
slice of all, she ran to the window, shouting angrily. Miggle
disappeared at once and ran home at top speed. He was afraid
of Mother Tick-Tock.

But he couldn't forget that wonderful Treacle-Jug. To think of
having rich sweet treacle at any time!
How lucky Mother Tick-Tock's
children were. No wonder he so
often saw them about with thick
slices of bread and treacle.

Now two days later Miggle made
himself a fine pudding. But when he

came to taste it he found that he had left out the sugar.
Oooh—how horrid it was!

"Now, if only I could borrow that Treacle-Jug!" thought
Miggle, longingly. "I could have treacle all over my pudding
and it would be one of the nicest I'd ever had. I wonder if
Mother Tick-Tock would lend me the jug."

Just at that very moment Miggle saw someone passing his
cottage, and who should it be but Mother Tick-Tock herself,
on her way to visit her friend, Mrs. Know-A-Lot. Miggle
watched her go down the road, and a small thought uncurled
itself in his mind.

"Couldn't I just borrow the Treacle-Jug for a few minutes?
Nobody would ever know. And if it's a magic jug, the treacle
would never, never come to an end, so it wouldn't matter my
having just a very little!"

He sat and thought about it, looking at his sugarless pudding.
Then he popped it back into the oven to keep warm, and ran
out of the front door very quickly indeed. "I must get that
jug before I change my mind!" he thought. "I'll use it to
cover my pudding with treacle, then I'll take it straight back.
Run, Miggle, run!"

He came to Mother Tick-Tock's cottage. The door was locked, but the window was open just a crack—a big enough crack for a small goblin to put in a bony little arm and reach on to a shelf for a small purple jug! There! He had got it. But how strange—it was quite empty!

"I'd better not go too fast with it, in case I fall and break it," he thought. So he put it under his coat and walked back slowly. He felt very excited indeed.

He stood the purple jug on his table and fetched his pudding from the oven. "Ha, pudding—you're going to taste very nice in a minute!" he said, and set it down in the middle of his table. He picked up the jug and spoke to it solemnly, just as Mother Tick-Tock had.

> "Pour me treacle, strong and sweet,
> For a Very Special Treat!"

said Miggle. The little jug left his hand at once and poised itself over the pudding. It tilted—and to Miggle's great delight a stream of rich golden treacle poured out and fell on his pudding. Miggle's mouth began to water. Ooooh! That pudding was going to taste very very nice!

"There! That's enough, thank you, little Treacle-Jug," said Miggle at last. "Don't pour any more, or the treacle will spill out of the dish."

But the jug took no notice at all. It went on pouring steadily, and Miggle saw that the treacle was now dripping over the edges of the pudding-dish. "Hey! Didn't you hear what I said!" he cried. "Stop, jug! You'll ruin my tablecloth!"

But the jug didn't stop. It still hung there in the air, treacle pouring from its little spout. Miggle was angry. He snatched at the jug, but it hopped away in the air and went on pouring in another place.

" *Stop*, jug ! Don't pour treacle into my armchair ! "
shouted Miggle. " Oh my goodness, look what you've done !
Emptied treacle all over the seat of my chair and the cushion !
Come away from there ! "

He snatched at the jug again, but it wouldn't let itself be
caught. It got away from his grabbing hand just in time and
hung itself up in the air just above the wash-tub, which was
full of Miggle's dirty clothes, soaking in the suds there.

" Hey ! " cried Miggle in alarm. " Not over my washing,
for goodness' sake ! Stop, I say ! Don't you see what you're
doing ? You're not supposed to pour treacle over chairs and
wash-tubs, only over puddings and tarts. Oh, you mischievous
jug ! Wait till I get you ! I'll break you in half ! "

He snatched at the jug again, but it swung away in the air
and this time hung itself over the nice new hearth-rug.

Trickle, trickle, trickle—the rich, sticky treacle poured
down steadily over the rug, and poor Miggle tried to pull it
away. But he soon found himself standing in treacle, for it
spread gradually over the floor.

Then Miggle began to feel very alarmed indeed. What was he to do with this mad Treacle-Jug? He simply MUST stop it somehow.

"Ah—I've an idea!" thought Miggle. "Where's my fishing-net? I'll get that and catch the jug in it. Then I'll smash it to bits on the ground. Oh, this treacle! How I hate walking in it! It's just like glue!"

He made his way to the corner where he kept his net and took hold of it. At once the Treacle-Jug swung itself over to him and poured treacle down on his head and face. How horrible! How sticky! Miggle was so angry that he shouted at the top of his voice.

"I'll smash you! I'll break you into a hundred pieces!" He swung the fishing-net at the jug and almost caught it. It seemed frightened and swung away out of the door and up the stairs, pouring treacle all the way. Miggle sat down and cried bitterly. Whatever was he to do?

Soon he heard a curious glug-glug noise, and he looked up

in alarm. A river of treacle was flowing slowly down the stairs! It flowed through the kitchen and out of the door, down the path and into the street. People passing by were quite astonished.

Mother Tick-Tock, coming back from visiting her friend, was astonished too. But she knew in a trice what had happened.

" Miggle's borrowed my Treacle-Jug ! " she said. " I saw him peeping through the window when I used it the other night. The mean, thieving little fellow ! "

Miggle saw Mother Tick-Tock and waded out through the treacly river to his front gate, crying, " Please, Mother Tick-Tock, I'm sorry. I can't make the jug stop pouring. Is there a spell to stop it as well as to start it ? "

" Of course there is," said Mother Tick-Tock. " It's just as well to know *both* spells if you steal something like a Treacle-Jug, Miggle. Well, you can keep the jug if you like. I've a much bigger one I can use. How tired of treacle you must be, Miggle ! "

" Oh, Mother Tick-Tock, please, please take your jug away," begged Miggle, kneeling down in the treacle. " I'll do anything you say, if only you will ! "

" Very well. If you come and dig my garden for me all the year round and keep it nice, I'll stop the jug from pouring. and take it back," said Mother Tick-Tock. Miggle groaned. He did so hate gardening !

" I'll come," he said. " I don't want to, but I will."

" If you don't, I'll send the jug to pour over your head," said Mother Tick-Tock, and everyone laughed. She called loudly, " Treacle-Jug, come here ! "

The little purple jug sailed out of a bedroom window and hung over Miggle's head. He dodged away at once. Mother Tick-Tock chanted loudly,

> " Be empty, jug, and take yourself
> Back to your place upon my shelf ! "

And—hey presto—the Treacle-Jug became quite empty, turned itself upside-down to show Mother Tick-Tock that it had obeyed her, and then flew swiftly through the air on the way to her cottage. Mother Tick-Tock knew she would find it standing quietly in its place on her kitchen-shelf.

" Well, goodbye, Miggle," she said. " You've quite a lot of cleaning up to do, haven't you ? Somehow I don't think you'll want to eat treacle again in a hurry ! "

She was right. Poor old Miggle can't even *see* a treacle-tin now without running for miles ! And I'm not a bit surprised at that !

The Little Sugar-Mouse

ONCE there was a little sugar-mouse. He was made of pink sugar, and he had two eyes, two ears, and a long pink tail. He belonged to Eileen, and she wouldn't eat him.

"He's rather a dear," she said to her mother. "I like the way he looks at me. I shan't eat him, Mummy. He's quite the nicest mouse I've ever seen."

Goodness! How grand the sugar-mouse felt when he heard that. He sat on the window-seat with the other toys, looking as important as he could. He was the nicest sugar-mouse ever seen, he kept thinking to himself. Fancy that!

The other toys thought he was a funny little mouse. The big doll wanted him for a pet. The golliwog wanted to cuddle him. The teddy-bear wanted to stroke him.

But the sugar-mouse was vain and haughty. He thought himself very grand and important. So he was rude when the other toys were nice to him.

"Leave me alone," he said to the bear, when the bear tried to stroke him. "I'm not a dog!"

"Please don't try to cuddle me," he said to the golliwog, when Golly wanted to pick him up. "I'm not a baby. Go to the dolls' house and get a doll from there if you want something to cuddle."

"I will certainly not be a pet," he said to the big doll, when she wanted to take him on her knee. "I am a grand and most important mouse—the nicest mouse Eileen has ever seen, she says!"

The toys grew tired of the sugar-mouse's high-and-mighty ways. They wouldn't talk to him any more. Then he was cross, because he wanted to talk to them and keep telling them what a wonderful little mouse he was. He wanted them to say so, too.

So when they wouldn't talk to him, he became very naughty and mischievous. He waited till the teddy-bear was rather near the edge of the window-seat, and then he ran at him with his sharp little sugar nose. He pushed the bear—and Teddy slid to the floor below with a bump. He was too fat to climb up again by himself, and he was very cross to hear the sugar-mouse giggling away to himself above.

The sugar-mouse annoyed the big doll too. He waited till she was asleep, with her eyes tight-shut, and then he undid her shoe-laces and all the buttons on her frock. She was really very puzzled.

"Every time I go to sleep my shoe-laces and buttons are done up properly," she said, "and everytime I wake they are all undone. Sugar-mouse, if it is you playing this trick, I shall be very cross."

But the worst trick of all the sugar-mouse played on the golliwog. Golly had a shock of black hair all over his head, and he was very proud of it because it was so thick and black. Well, the sugar-mouse saw the tin of flour on the window-sill, where Mummy had put it for a moment. And he climbed up the tin, picked up a whole heap of the white flour in his sugar-paws, and threw it down on the golly's head. And in a trice the golliwog had white hair instead of black. The toys stared at him in horror.

" Golly ! You've gone white ! " said the doll.

" Golly ! Have you grown old suddenly ? " said the bear. " Your hair is all white, as if you were an old, old golliwog."

The sugar-mouse gave a giggle and nearly fell into the flour-tin. The toys looked up.

" Oh ! It's that tiresome sugar-mouse again ! " cried the golliwog. " Wait till I catch him ! I'll bury him in the flour till he can't breathe."

But the sugar-mouse was too quick for him. He hid in the brick-box and wouldn't come out till the toys were good-tempered again.

Then the toys made up their minds that they simply could NOT let the sugar-mouse go anywhere with them. Sometimes they all went for a walk round the nursery at night, and the mouse loved to trot along behind, looking at everything they

passed—the big coal-scuttle, the dancing fire, the dolls' house in the corner, and the enormous rocking-horse.

Sometimes the toys even went into the garden—and that was a very great treat. Often they went out of the nursery door if it had been left open, and walked down the passage to peep into the big kitchen.

And now the sugar-mouse was not allowed to go with them at all. The toys slipped off when he was asleep. He was very angry indeed. He made up his mind that he WOULD go with them the very next time.

Well, the next time they went, it was raining. The toys badly wanted to go into the garden because the big doll had a little umbrella, and both the teddy and the golly had mackintoshes and sou'westers of their own. Eileen had bought them for them at the toy-shop, and they had never worn them in the rain.

" I'm coming too," said the sugar-mouse, when he saw them putting on their rain-things.

" You are not," said the big doll. " It's raining. Don't be silly. Sugar-mice never go out in the wet."

" Well, *I* shall," said the sugar-mouse. " Anyway, why shouldn't sugar-mice go out in the wet, if you do ? You are just making that up."

" No, I'm not," said the big doll. " I've always heard it said that sugar-mice never go out in the wet, but I don't really know why that is. Anyway, don't be silly, sugar-mouse—we don't want you with us, and it's dangerous for you to go out in the wet. I'm sure it is."

" Well, I'm coming," said the sugar-mouse, and he ran along behind the doll with her umbrella, and the teddy and the golly in their mackintoshes and sou'westers. They tried to make him go back, but he wouldn't. He was really very naughty. He pinched the big doll very hard, and he trod in a puddle and splashed the teddy from head to foot. They were very cross with him.

It was raining hard when they got out into the garden. The doll didn't mind because she had her umbrella. The teddy and the golly were as dry as could be, and very proud indeed of their mackintoshes. The bear's sou'wester kept falling down over his nose, so that he couldn't see, but he didn't really mind that. The raindrops fell, plop, plop, plop, on to the sugar-mouse, who had no umbrella, no mackintosh, and no sou'-wester. At first he thought it was rather fun. Then he thought he didn't like it very much. He began to squeak.

The toys turned round and stared at him.

" What is wrong with the sugar-mouse ? " asked the big doll in alarm. " He's going small."

" His eyes don't look at me any more," said the golly.

" His sugar-paws have gone," said the bear.

" Oh, please, I don't feel at all well," said the sugar-mouse in a little frightened voice. "Pet me, Big Doll. Cuddle me, Golly. Stroke me, Bear. Be kind to me, please."

Well, the toys were kind-hearted, so they went to pick up the sugar-mouse and comfort him. But they couldn't pick him up. He was going smaller—and smaller—and smaller!

And very soon he was gone altogether. The toys stared in dismay.

"Where has he gone?" said the big doll. "We must take him home quickly. Where has he gone?"

"Sugar-mouse, where have you gone?" cried the bear.

But there was no answer. There never would be. The silly, vain, mischievous little sugar-mouse had melted in the rain! What a pity!

Only his tail was left. The big doll carried it sadly back to the nursery and put it on the window-seat. There Eileen found it the next day—but no sugar-mouse was there with the little tail.

"Somebody's eaten him!" cried Eileen, almost in tears. "Oh, who ate my dear little sugar-mouse?"

"The rain ate him," said the big doll in a whisper. "The rain ate him, Eileen. Oh, what a pity!"

Jimmy and the Jackdaw

ONCE there was a boy called Jimmy. When he had a birthday his uncle gave him a book all about birds.

There were pictures of birds in it and pictures of birds' eggs, too.

" Aren't they pretty ! " Jimmy said to his friend Connie. " Look at this picture of hedge-sparrows' eggs—they are as blue as the sky. I've a good mind to look for a hedge-sparrow's nest and take the eggs for myself."

" Oh, you mustn't do that," said Connie at once. " It isn't kind to take the eggs out of a bird's nest. You know you mustn't do it."

Jimmy didn't listen. It was springtime, and many birds were building their nests. Jimmy saw them flying here and there with bits of straw, or a feather, in their beaks.

" I shall look out for a hedge-sparrow's nest and take the eggs," thought Jimmy. " I shall put the eggs into a box lined with cotton-wool. No one will know."

Well, he did find a hedge-sparrow's nest. It was in the hawthorn hedge that ran beside the lane. Jimmy saw the bird fly into it, and he tiptoed to the hedge.

He parted the sprays and peeped into the heart of the hedge. At first he couldn't see the nest, and then he suddenly did. It was well tucked away, hidden by the green leaves.

And in the nest was the mother hedge-sparrow, sitting on her eggs, keeping them warm ! She looked at Jimmy, but she did not move.

" Fly away, fly away ! " said Jimmy, and he shook the hedge.

It was very unkind of him. The little brown bird was afraid. She flew up from her nest and perched on a nearby tree, watching anxiously.

Jimmy saw the pretty blue eggs there, four of them. He was so greedy that he took them all. He did not leave the little mother bird even one.

She was very unhappy. She flew back to her nest after Jimmy had gone and looked sadly into it. Where were her pretty, very precious eggs? They were gone. The little hedge-sparrow burst into a sad little song, and told the other birds around the dreadful thing that had so suddenly happened to her.

Jimmy went home with the eggs. They looked very pretty on the white cotton-wool in the box. They were so pretty that he thought he would like to draw and paint them. He was very, very good at drawing and painting.

" Now, where's my silver pencil ? " said Jimmy. " I can easily draw these eggs. I think I will draw a nest first and then draw the blue eggs inside."

Jimmy began to draw with his silver pencil. He was very proud of that pencil, because he had won it at school as a drawing prize. No other boy had a silver pencil. Jimmy felt grand when he took it out of his pocket at school to use it.

The next nest he found was a robin's. It was built on the ground under a hedge on Jimmy's own garden. There were four eggs in it, and Jimmy took them all. The robin made an angry clicking noise at him, but she couldn't stop him. She was very sad, and flew away from her nest, making up her mind that she would never build or sing in Jimmy's garden again.

Jimmy went on collecting eggs. He only told Connie about them, and wanted to show them to her, but she wouldn't look.

"I think you are bad and unkind," she said. "You are making a lot of birds unhappy. I don't like you."

One day Jimmy walked by the old ruined castle. He heard the sound of many birds crying "chack-chack-chack" and he looked up.

"What a lot of jackdaws!" he said to himself. "Oh—wouldn't I like some jackdaws' eggs! I know they build their nests up there in the old tower. I guess I could find some if I climbed up to see."

It wasn't very difficult for Jimmy to climb up to the castle tower. He found foot-holes in the crumbling stone, and made his way up little by little. Soon he found himself looking through a hole, inside which a jackdaw had built his enormous untidy nest of twigs.

And there, just within reach of Jimmy's hand, were three big eggs! "What a bit of luck!" said Jimmy, and he put out his hand to take them.

Soon he was climbing down the walls again, the eggs safely in his pocket. He hurried home, and found a box big enough to put the eggs in. He really had quite a fine collection now! He took all the eggs, every time he found a nest—he did not leave the mother-bird even one or two. He did not think once of her sadness when she found she had no eggs left to sit on.

The next day Jimmy was sitting in his room by the open window, drawing a map of England for his geography lesson. He was using his lovely bright silver pencil, of course.

He got up to fetch his ruler, and put his pencil down on the window-ledge. Just as he did this, a big bird, quite black except for a grey patch at the back of its head, came flying by.

It was a jackdaw. It saw the silver pencil shining in the sun, and it flew down to the sill at once. It loved bright things.

It picked the silver pencil up in its beak. It was heavy, but the jackdaw was a big, strong bird. Jimmy turned when he heard the flutter of wings.

He saw the jackdaw pick up his precious pencil. He saw him fly off with it in his beak! He saw him getting smaller and smaller as he flew right away to the castle tower, where he and the other jackdaws had their nests!

" Oh! " shouted Jimmy. " Oh! You wicked bird! You've stolen my pencil! Come back, come back! "

But the jackdaw didn't come back. He put it into his nest. He already had a piece of silver paper there and somebody's shining thimble. The pencil looked nice laid beside them.

Jimmy was terribly upset. He ran to the window and yelled. He began to cry, and the tears ran down his cheeks like two little streams. He was still crying when Connie came into his room.

" That jackdaw is a thief! " wailed Jimmy. " He has stolen my most precious thing—the silver pencil I loved."

Connie looked at Jimmy, and didn't say anything.

" Why don't you say something ? " cried Jimmy, wiping his tears. " You know how much I loved my pencil. I won it for a prize. Aren't you sorry it's gone ? It's most unfair of that jackdaw to come and take it like that."

" Well, I think it was fair, not unfair," said Connie, at last. " After all, Jimmy, the jackdaw was doing exactly the same thing that you did to him. You took his eggs—and he took your pencil."

" But I loved my pencil ! " cried Jimmy.

" Birds love their eggs," said Connie. " They wouldn't sit so long on them as they do, they wouldn't look so happy when they are sitting, if they didn't love their eggs. That little hedge-sparrow loved her eggs, but you took them. The robin loved hers, and you took them. The jackdaw did too, but you took those."

" But my pencil was made of silver and it was very precious,"
wept Jimmy.

" I expect birds' eggs are even more precious to them than
your silver pencil was to you," said Connie. " After all, eggs
have something alive inside them—baby birds. I expect they
are as precious to the bird as you are to your mother."

" Connie, be nice to me, I'm so unhappy," said Jimmy.

" I would be nice to you, if you could see that what has
happened is quite fair and just," said Connie. " You said the
jackdaw was wicked because he stole your pencil. Well, why
can't you see that you were bad to steal his eggs ? You do
horrid things yourself—but you don't like it when the same
kind of thing happens to you. And what is more, I don't think
the jackdaw is wicked, because *he* doesn't know that stealing is
wrong, and you do ! "

" Oh, Connie, I do see that it's fair and just," wept poor
Jimmy. " I do, I do. I won't take any more eggs. I was
greedy and horrid to take every egg I saw. I won't do it any
more. I know what it's like now to be without something I
love. Oh, I wish I hadn't been horrid."

Connie put her arms round him. " Don't cry," she said.
" I'll be nice to you now you say that. Perhaps I could buy
you a new pencil with the money out of my money-box."

" No, don't do that," said Jimmy, at once. " Perhaps the
jackdaw will bring my pencil back."

But he didn't. It is still in his nest. Poor Jimmy ! It was a
hard punishment, but a very fair one, wasn't it ?

Brownie Blackberries

Blackberries ! Blackberries ! Who will buy ?
Fine black juicy ones, fit for a pie,
Picked by the brownies at break of day,
Long before children come out to play.

Ho there, witches, the berries are cheap,
Cook them today, for they will not keep !
Ho there, pixies, now is your chance,
Make blackberry jelly for your next dance !

Hey, little elves, there are some left for you,
Mix them with sugar and silvery dew,
Blackberries, blackberries, fine and sweet,
Here I go selling them, all down the street !

The Poor Pink Pig

ONCE upon a time there was a fat pink pig who belonged to Mother Winkle. Mother Winkle was half a witch and she sometimes made spells, but she didn't really know very much about them, and so they often went wrong.

The pig was called Tubby, and Mother Winkle often used to call him into the kitchen to help her with her spells. She hadn't a green-eyed black cat to help her, as most real witches have—she couldn't afford one, for they were very dear to buy. But Tubby the pink pig did quite well instead.

Tubby hated having to help Mother Winkle. The spells smelt funny, and you never knew when green or yellow smoke would suddenly appear, or flames jump out of nothing. So he used to try to hide when he knew Mother Winkle was doing magic. It wasn't any good, though—Mother Winkle always found him. He was too fat to hide himself properly.

One day Mother Winkle shooed him into the kitchen to help her to do a new spell. Someone had given her a spell for Magic Cakes, and she wanted to make some. But to do that she had to get Tubby to stand in the middle of a circle of chalk whilst she stood outside and sang a lot of magic words.

Tubby didn't want to help, but he had to. He stood there in the middle of the chalk circle, looking very fat and miserable. Mother Winkle stood outside with her magic stick and book, and then she began to recite enchanted words in a sing-song voice.

In two minutes, to Tubby's enormous surprise, a great many small currant cakes suddenly appeared inside the chalk circle, just by him.

There they were, smelling new-baked and most delicious. Tubby's mouth watered and his nose twitched. How he longed to sniff at one of those cakes, but he didn't dare to move whilst the magic was going on.

Just as Mother Winkle put her book down to go and fetch a plate for the magic cakes, a knock came at the door.

"Bother! That's the butcher!" said Mother Winkle and went to the door, leaving Tubby and the cakes alone in the circle.

Well, that was too much for Tubby. As soon as Mother Winkle's back was turned he sniffed at a cake, and it smelt so good he ate it. My goodness me, it tasted good too! Tubby ate another—and another—and another! In fact, he had eaten nearly all of them when Mother Winkle came back!

And then Tubby noticed something very, very queer. Mother Winkle looked ENORMOUS! Simply ENORMOUS! He couldn't make it out. He looked round the room—and squealed in surprise. The chairs and the tables were enormous too!

Those magic cakes had a spell in them to make anyone who ate them grow much smaller! Tubby had eaten a lot and he was now very tiny. Each cake had made him half his size!

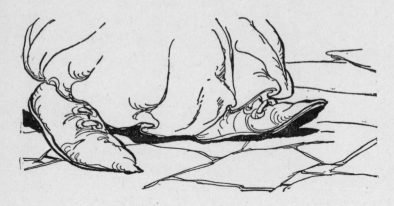

Mother Winkle stared at him in amazement, and then she stamped her foot in anger.

"Oh, you silly, greedy, stupid pig! You've eaten nearly all my magic cakes! You wicked creature! Wait till I make you your right size again, and I'll beat you with my stick till you squeal for mercy!"

Tubby was so frightened that he leapt out of the chalk circle and ran into a corner. Mother Winkle ran after him—and then the little pig discovered that it was much easier to hide himself now he was tiny ! He squeezed into a mouse-hole and stood quite still there. Mother Winkle poked here and there under the chairs but she couldn't find him anywhere.

Tubby squeezed himself still further back in the mouse-hole—and found himself against something warm and soft.

" Hallo, hallo ! " said a squeaky voice. " Who are you ? "

Tubby turned and saw a little brown mouse with bright black eyes.

" I hope I'm not in your way," he said politely. " But the truth is I'm trying to hide from that horrid person Mother Winkle. She is going to beat me."

" Dear, dear ! " said the mouse, shaking his head in dismay. " I'm sorry for you, I really am. She is not a nice person. She is mean. She never leaves a single crumb out for me or my family. Why don't you run away ? "

" That's a fine idea ! " said Tubby, in delight. " Why should I ever go back ? Oh, but, mouse—there's one thing I had forgotten—I'm too tiny. Who will make me a big, proper pig again, if I don't go back to Mother Winkle ? "

" No one will," said the mouse, cheerfully. " But why do you want to be a big, proper pig ? It's much nicer to be small. I've been small all my life and it suits me very well. You can hide beautifully, and creep anywhere you like. I should keep small if I were you, Piggy-wig."

Tubby thought about it, and he decided that the mouse was right. It would be nice to be small.

" But I must find a home somewhere," he said to the mouse. " I must belong to someone."

" Well, creep through my hole," said the mouse. " I'll show you where it leads to. It leads to a farm, and you can ask the

farmer's wife if she will keep you for her own pig. She is very kind to all animals. I expect she will let you live on her farm."

So Tubby followed the kind little mouse through the long tunnel, and at last came up into a field. The mouse poked his head out to see if any of the cats were about, but none was to be seen.

"There's the farmer's wife, look!" whispered the mouse. "Feeding her chickens—do you see? Go and ask her now."

Tubby said goodbye to the mouse and hurried over to the farmer's wife. He squeaked up at her from the ground and she suddenly saw him among her hens, looking very small indeed, tinier than the tiniest chick. She picked him up in astonishment.

"Will you give me a home?" squeaked Tubby. "I have run away, and I want a new home."

The farmer's wife laughed and shook her head.

"You funny little creature!" she said. "You wouldn't be any good to me! You're too small! The other pigs would gobble you up. No, no, you must go somewhere else!"

Tubby scampered away. He was sad. Where should he go now? He wandered on and on and at last came to a hillside where sheep, looking as large as elephants, were all busily eating the grass.

"I'd like to live out here on the hillside," thought Tubby. "There's plenty of sunshine, and the sheep wouldn't take any notice of me. I'll go and ask the shepherd if he'll have me."

So he went to where the shepherd was sitting on the grass, looking at the sky to see if rain was coming.

" Will you have me for your own ? " squeaked the pig to the surprised shepherd. " I'm a pig run away from home. I'm a real pig, but very small."

The shepherd threw back his head and laughed.

" Who wants a tiny pig like you ! " he said. " You're no use to anyone. My dogs would smell you out and nibble you. Go away whilst there's time."

The poor pink pig scampered off in a hurry, looking behind him to see if the sheep-dogs were coming. He went on until he came to a goose-girl, taking her geese on to the common. He ran up to her and tugged at the lace in her shoe.

" Let me be your pig ! " he squeaked. " Let me live with your geese ! "

The goose-girl looked at him in astonishment.

" But what use are you ? " she asked. " Such a little thing as you are ! Who wants a pig as tiny as you ! "

The geese saw the tiny pig and began to hiss and cackle. They crowded round Tubby and he was frightened. He slipped between their yellow legs and ran off as fast as he could.

He hid himself all day, afraid of cats, dogs and geese. When night came he set out once more, and soon came to a big house. He squeezed himself under the door and went in. The first room he came to was a nursery. There were dolls on a shelf, a ball on the floor, a clockwork engine in a cupboard with soldiers and a kite, and, just by the wall, a big Noah's Ark.

Everyone was surprised to see the pink pig.

" Are you a toy ? " asked the biggest doll.

" No, I'm a proper pig, but very small," said the pig.

He told the toys all his adventures, and they were sorry for him. All the animals in the Noah's Ark came out to look at him. There were two elephants, two bears, two lions, two tigers, two cows, two goats, two chickens, two ducks—in fact, two of everything.

No—not quite two of everything, after all. There was only one pig, a little black one. He ran over to Tubby and had a good look at him.

" Oh ! " he said. " I really thought at first that you were the other Noah's Ark pig come back again. You know, he was left out of the ark one day, on the carpet—and when the housemaid swept up the next morning, she swept the little pig into her dust-pan, and we never saw him again."

"We think he must have been put into the dust-bin with the rubbish and taken away," said the biggest doll, sadly. " We missed him very much. You are rather like him."

" I am very lonely without him," said the black Noah's Ark pig. " I suppose, little live pig, you wouldn't like to be a toy and live with us in the ark ? We have great fun, for the children often take us out and walk us all round the floor. You would be well taken care of, too, and we would all be friends with you."

Well, can you imagine how delighted Tubby was ! He rubbed his nose against the black pig's nose and squealed for joy.

" Of course I'll live with you ! " he cried. " I'd love to ! I don't want to be big any more. I like being little. And oh, it will be such fun living with so many animals. But, little black pig, you are sure the lions and bears won't eat me ? "

" Oh goodness me, no ! " said the black pig. " They are made of wood. They are not alive, like you. You will have to pretend to be made of wood too, when the children play with us."

" Oh, I can easily do that ! " said Tubby. He climbed back into the ark with all the others, and settled down for the night. He was so pleased to have found such a nice home. The ark was warm and comfortable, and the other animals were friendly and jolly. He was very happy.

But when the children, Anne and Margaret, played with their Noah's Ark animals next day, how surprised they were !

" Margaret ! Here's another little pig instead of the one we lost ! " cried Anne, picking up Tubby. " Oh, isn't he

nice and fat! He looks so real too. I wonder who put him there."

Nobody knew. Mother didn't know, nor did Daddy. Nurse shook her head and so did Jane the housemaid. Nobody knew at all. You can't *think* how puzzled they all were!

Tubby still lives in the Noah's Ark—and I'd *love* to tell Anne and Margaret how he got there, wouldn't you?

The Peeping Pixie

Oh little pixie there,
The sun upon your shining hair,
How big the world must seem!
A dewdrop trembling in the grass
For you becomes a looking-glass,
Alight with rainbow gleam.

A kindly daisy gives you shade,
A beetle makes you quite afraid,
And spiders peer like witches!
Petals that the rose flung down
You've made into a velvet gown—
And oh, what tiny stitches!

Our clumsy giant-feet you dread,
That shake your coach of spider-thread,
And tumble you in fear,
Oh peeping pixie, stay with me,
So soft and gentle I will be,
To you, my little dear.

One Rainy Night

ONE dark night two fairies set out to go to a party. They had on new frocks, made of buttercup petals, so the two little creatures shone as bright as gold as they ran through the night.

But they hadn't gone very far before it began to rain. They looked at one another in dismay.

" Our new frocks will be spoilt ! " said Linnie.

" We shall be soaked through and to-morrow we shall sneeze and have a cold," said Denny. They crouched under a bush and waited. But the rain went on and on.

Presently the two fairies heard voices, and they listened. " It's the toys playing in Doreen's nursery," said Linnie. " That means that everyone has gone to bed. Let's fly in at the window and see if they can lend us a towel to dry ourselves."

So they flew in at the nursery window. The toys were very pleased to see them.

"I say! Aren't you wet!" cried the teddy-bear. "Is it raining?"

"Of course!" said Linnie. "Did you think we had been bathing in a puddle or something?"

The toys laughed. The golliwog went to get a towel out of the dolls'-house bathroom. Soon the two fairies were rubbing themselves dry.

" Where are you going to, all dressed up in buttercup gold ? " asked the curly-haired doll.

" To a party ! " said Linnie. " But it's a long way away—and we shall get wet through as soon as we fly out of the window again. It really is a nuisance. I suppose, Curly-haired Doll, you haven't two old coats you could lend us ? "

The curly-haired doll got excited. " I tell you what I and the straight-haired doll *have* got ! " she said. " We have each got mackintoshes and sou'-westers ! Doreen had them in her stocking for Christmas, and we wore them when we went out in the rain. They would just fit you two ! "

" Oh, do lend them to us ! " begged Linnie. So the curly-haired doll went to get them. But they were hanging up high on a peg, and none of the toys could reach them. The two fairies flew up and got them. Then they put them on, and they really did look nice in them ! One mackintosh was red and the other was blue.

" I suppose it's all right borrowing them without telling Doreen ? " said the teddy-bear. " You know, I heard some-one say the other day that nobody should ever borrow anything without asking first. And we haven't asked Doreen."

" Well—let's go and ask her then," said Linnie. The toys stared at her in surprise.

" We can't do *that* ! " said the bear. " Why, Doreen would be awfully surprised if we woke her up and spoke to her in the middle of the night ! "

" But wouldn't she think it was a *nice* surprise ? " said Denny. The toys looked at one another. The golly nodded his head.

" Yes," he said, " I believe she would. She is always saying that she wishes we were alive. Well—shall *I* go and ask her—or will you, Denny and Linnie ? "

Helen Jacobs

"You toys had better go," said Linnie. So all the toys went trotting out of the nursery door, across the landing, to Doreen's bedroom. She was fast asleep in her bed, and the bear wondered how to wake her up. He found her hand outside the sheet and patted it. She didn't wake. Then the golliwog tugged at the sheet, and that did wake her !

She sat up and switched on her light. She stared in astonishment at the toys. "I must be dreaming !" she said. "Look at all my toys standing by my bed !"

"No. You're not dreaming," said the bear. "We woke you up to ask you something, Doreen. There are two fairies who want to borrow the new mackintoshes and sou'-westers belonging to the dolls. It's such a rainy night and they are on their way to a party. We didn't like to lend them anything without asking first."

" Quite right," said Doreen, getting out of bed. " I really must see these fairies ! Where are they ? "

" In the nursery," said the bear, and they all went back with Doreen. She gazed in delight at the two fairies in their golden frocks and mackintoshes.

" What lovely things you are ! " she said. " Oh dear—I wonder if this is a dream ! To see my toys alive and to see fairies, all in one night, is just too good to be true ! "

" Thank you for saying we may borrow these things," said Linnie. " We'll go now—and we'll hang them safely on the pegs when we come back ! "

They flew out of the window, looking really sweet in the mackintoshes and sou'-westers. The toys waved good-bye. Doreen went back to bed and fell asleep again.

At cockcrow Linnie and Denny came back, after a perfectly lovely party. It was not raining now, so they could go home safely. They flew in at the window and hung the mackintoshes and sou'-westers on the pegs. The toys were all back in the toy-cupboard and did not stir.

" I wish we could say thank you to Doreen," said Linnie. " I wonder how we could."

"I know!" cried Denny, seeing a box of letters in the cupboard. "Look—there are lots of letters in that box! Let's spell the words 'THANK YOU' in letters and put them on the table. Then Doreen will see them in the morning and know we have thanked her for her kindness!"

So they spelt the words 'THANK YOU' in letters on the table and then flew out of the window. And in the morning, when Doreen came into the nursery, she found the words there, and she stared in surprise.

"Look, Mother!" she said. "Isn't that funny? 'THANK YOU!' Who put it there, and why, I wonder?"

Then she went red in delight, and cried out joyfully, "Oh, *I* know! Of course! It was the two fairies who said thank you! Oh, Mother, I thought last night that I dreamt my toys came to wake me up to ask me to lend two dear little fairies my dolls' mackintoshes—but it wasn't a dream after all! Dreams can't say THANK YOU, can they!"

"I shouldn't think so," said Mother. "Well, well—fancy you talking to toys and fairies in the middle of the night, Doreen! Whatever will you do next!"

"I Don't Want To!"

ONCE upon a time there was a little girl called Fanny. She was eight years old, and she had been spoilt. She had been ill quite a lot, and because her mother had been sorry for her, she had let Fanny have her own way far too much.

Whenever she asked Fanny to do something she didn't like, the little girl would say " I don't want to ! " and would pout and frown.

" Will you go and post this letter for me ? " her mother would say. And Fanny would make the usual answer :

" I don't want to ! "

Well, if you say a thing like that often enough, you just can't stop, and soon Fanny was saying "I don't want to!" a hundred times a day.

"What a spoilt child!" people said. "Really she is most unpleasant!"

Her Granny spoke sternly to her. "Fanny," she said, "I don't like this habit you have of saying 'I don't want to!' to everything. Do try to stop."

"I don't want to," said Fanny at once.

Well, well—what can you do with a child like that!

Now one day Fanny went across the fields and took a wrong turning. Soon she found herself outside a queer little house. A well stood nearby and an old woman was turning the handle that drew up the bucket of water. She saw Fanny and beckoned to her.

" Little girl, come and help me to get this water ! "
" I don't want to ! " said Fanny at once.

The old woman frowned. She wound up the bucket, took
it off the hook, and set it down.

" You could carry it for me into the house," she said. " I'm
rather tired to-day."

" I don't want to ! " said Fanny, of course.

" Well, what a horrid child ! " said the old dame. " You
can't seem to say anything else but ' I don't want to ! ' Can't
you say something pleasant for a change ? "

" I don't want to ! " said Fanny.

"Very well—don't!" said the old woman. "Say 'I don't want
to !' and nothing else ! Maybe you will soon want to change !"

And with that she went up the path to her cottage, opened
the door, went inside and shut the door after her. Fanny felt a
bit frightened. She remembered that the old woman had green
eyes. Perhaps she was one of the fairy folk !

She ran off, and soon found her path. She went back home—and on the way she met Jane, a school-friend.

"Fanny! Come and play with me after tea and see my new doll!" called Jane.

"I don't want to!" said Fanny, much to her own surprise, because she did want to, very much indeed. Jane had told everyone at school about her new doll, which could stand up by itself, and say "Mamma!"

"All right, don't come then!" said Jane, offended. "I'll ask Mary."

Fanny walked home, upset. Her mother met her at the door.

"Fanny dear, go and get yourself some sweets before you come in," she said. "You didn't have your Saturday sixpence last week. Go and spend it now."

"I don't want to!" said Fanny, and made her mother stare in surprise. Fanny stared at her mother too. She hadn't meant to say that! She loved sweets and it was fun to go and buy them. She wanted to say "I *do* want to!" but all her tongue said was "I don't want to!" once again.

"My dear child, if you don't want to, you needn't!" said her mother. "How tiresome you are sometimes! I will give your sixpence to John next door."

Fanny walked up to her bedroom, almost in tears. She passed the cook on the way.

"I'm making cakes," said Cook. "Come along down and scrape the dishes out, Miss Fanny."

Now this was a thing that Fanny simply loved doing. But, as you can guess, all her tongue would answer was "I don't want to!"

"Well, I thought it would be a treat for you," said the cook, offended, and she marched downstairs with her head in the air.

Poor Fanny! This was a dreadful day for her. It seemed as

if everyone was offering something nice for her to do. And all she could say was " I don't want to ! "

In the end everyone was cross with her, and her mother sent her to bed. " Go up to bed and stay there ! " said Mummy.

" I don't want to ! " said Fanny. But she had to go all the same.

Now when she was in bed, crying under the clothes, there came a tap at the door—and who should come in but the old woman who had been by the well.

" Good evening," she said to Fanny. " How have you been getting on with that tongue of yours ? Wouldn't it be nice to speak properly again ? "

Fanny couldn't answer, because she knew that if she did, her tongue would say " I don't want to ! " And she did badly want to speak properly again—very, very badly.

" Well now," said the old dame. " I'll make a bargain with you. If you try to be a nice little girl, and will not be spoilt

and rude, I'll make your tongue right again. But I warn you that if you say ' I don't want to ' more than once in a day, the spell will come back again and you'll find you can't say anything else but that ! "

" Thank you," said Fanny. " I'm sorry I was rude to you. I won't be rude or spoilt any more."

" That's the way to talk ! " said the old dame, and she smiled. " Good-bye ! Come and see me another day, and maybe your tongue will say something nicer to me than ' I don't want to ! ' "

Well, Fanny found it very hard to get out of her bad habit, but as she knew quite well that the spell would come back if she said " I don't want to " more than once in a day, she was very, very careful. The spell hasn't come back, so maybe she will be all right now.

She is trying to find the old woman's cottage again to tell her that she has cured herself. I wish I could go with her. I'd like to see the old dame's green eyes twinkling at me, wouldn't you ?

Well Done, Bob-Along!

WHENEVER anyone in Brownie Town had a party they always went shopping at Mr. Knobbly's shop. He was a brownie with bright green eyes and such bony hands and arms and legs that really Mr. Knobbly was a very good name for him.

" Everything for parties ! " Mr. Knobbly would call out when any of the Little Folk went by. " Balloons of all colours, big and bouncy, blown up as large as you like. Funny hats for everyone—buy a bonnet for Mr. Grumble, buy a dunce's hat for the schoolmaster ! Crackers to pull with the biggest BANG you ever heard ! "

It was a lovely shop to wander round. Balloons bumped against your head, pretty lanterns swung to and fro, funny hats could be tried on, and shining ornaments glittered everywhere.

All the same nobody liked Mr. Knobbly very much. He was a cheat, and when anybody ordered two dozen balloons, he would send only twenty-two or twenty-three, and hope that nobody would bother to count them. And often some of his crackers had nothing in them, and that was very disappointing indeed.

One day Mr. Knobbly was very, very pleased. Mr. Popple, the richest brownie in the town, was giving a big party for his little girl, Peronal, and, of course, he had been to order a great many things from Mr. Knobbly's shop.

" I want one hundred balloons," he said. " And twelve boxes of gay crackers, each with a nice little present inside.

And one hundred funny hats, with strong elastic for each one, so that the children can keep them on easily. I'll pay you well, so be sure and see that everything is first-class."

"Certainly, Mr. Popple, sir, certainly," said Mr. Knobbly, too delighted for words. "When is this party, sir?"

"In one week's time," said Mr. Popple. "All the balloons must be blown up very big, and have nice long strings, and be delivered on the morning of the party, so that they can be hung up all round the room."

Mr. Knobbly was soon very, very busy. He made a great many funny hats, and indeed he was very clever at that. But he wasn't going to put good strong elastic on them—oh no—strong elastic was expensive—he would get very cheap stuff. Nobody would notice!

"And I'm not going to put presents into each cracker,

either," said Mr. Knobbly to himself. " Often when a cracker is pulled, the present is shot out and goes under the table or somewhere ! If a cracker has no present in it, the child will think it's flown right out and go to look for it. He won't know that he'll never find it because it wasn't there ! Ha, ha—I'm a wily brownie, I am ! " It was when he came to blow up the balloons that he found himself in difficulties.

He didn't mind blowing up a dozen, he had often done that —but a hundred ! He looked at the piles of flat rubber, all balloons waiting to be blown up, and he shook his head.

" No—I can't do it. I'll have to get someone in to help." So he put a notice in his window.

WANTED
SOMEONE TO BLOW UP
BALLOONS

That day a small, rather raggedy brownie came by. He went about doing odd jobs, and he was a merry, honest little fellow that everybody liked. He saw the notice and popped his head round the door. " I can blow up balloons," he said. " I've plenty of very good breath, available at any moment of the day. I can also put a whistle into any balloon when I blow it up."

" What do you mean ? " said Knobbly, surprised.

" Well, I whistle as I blow," said the brownie, "and naturally, when I fill a balloon with my breath and whistle at the same time, the whistle goes into the balloon too—and when it's going down, as balloons do sooner or later, it whistles to warn the owner to blow it up again ! "

" How extraordinary ! " said Knobbly, thinking that he could certainly charge extra for Whistling Balloons. " All right, you can have the job. What's your name ? "

" Bob-Along," said the brownie. " And I'm as honest as the day, as anyone will tell you. What will you pay me ? "

" Depends on your work," said Knobbly. " Now look— fasten elastic on these hats for me, before you begin on the balloons."

Bob-Along fixed elastic on a clown's hat and then popped it on. But the elastic broke at once.

" Hey, " said Bob-Along, " this elastic's no good. Give me stronger pieces."

" You just do as you're told," said Knobbly, who was busy making crackers. Bob-Along picked one up. It was very pretty indeed. He shook it.

" Nothing inside ! " he said, and took a toy and pushed it into the cracker.

" You stop that," said Knobbly crossly. " I'm doing the crackers ! "

Bob-Along watched him. " Well, you're not doing them

very well," he said, after a minute or two. "You've missed putting toys into two more crackers. Better let me put the toys in for you, while you make them."

"You blow up the balloons," said Knobbly, getting tired of being watched by this bright-eyed brownie. "Another word from you and I'll kick you out of my shop!"

"You won't," said Bob-Along. "You haven't any breath to blow up your balloons! I've plenty! I'll start on them now, whistle and all!"

Well, Bob-Along certainly did know how to blow up balloons steadily and well. He whistled as he blew, and showed Knobbly how his whistle came out of the balloon again when he let the air out of it. It was really very peculiar. Knobbly was pleased, and decided to charge even more for them than he had planned at first.

More and more balloons were blown up by Bob-Along, and he tied each one's neck with string, and hung it to a pole, so that it did not get entangled with the others. Soon there were thirty hanging up, bobbing about gaily.

"Shall I shake each cracker for you, and see if you've left out any toys?" asked Bob-Along. "I want a rest from blowing now. I never blow up more than thirty balloons at a time, in case I use up all my breath."

"Don't be silly," said Knobbly. "If you feel like that you can come back tomorrow—but they'll *have* to be finished then, because that's the day of the party."

Bob-Along finished all the balloons the next day, and then, as Knobbly bade him, took them to Mr. Popple's big house. Mr. Popple was very, very pleased with such big ones, especially when he knew that a whistle had been blown into each one. Then Bob-Along went back to Knobbly's.

"I want my money now, please," he said.

"Here you are—fourpence," said Knobbly, and threw the pennies on the table.

"What—fourpence for my excellent work!" cried Bob-Along. "I want two shillings—and that's cheap for what I did."

"You'll take fourpence or nothing," said Knobbly, making the last cracker.

"Then I'll take nothing—except what I've put into your balloons!" said Bob-Along, and marched out.

"Hey—what do you mean?" cried Knobbly, but Bob-Along didn't answer. He went straight to Mr. Popple's and slipped into the party room, where the hundred balloons swung and swayed.

He untied the neck of first one and then another. The air came out with a loud whistle and the balloons went flat. Then Bob-Along undid three more, and again the air came out whistling. Mr. Popple heard the noise and came running in. "Look here—what are you doing?" he cried. "You've blown all those up—why are you making them flat again? You've been paid for that work!"

"No, I haven't," said Bob-Along. "Knobbly offered me fourpence, and I wouldn't take such a poor sum. So I've come to take away my breath—the breath I put into each balloon, and the whistle too. They're mine—my breath and my whistle—and if I'm not going to be paid for them, I'll have them back!"

"You dishonest fellow!" cried Mr. Popple.

c

"Oh no, I'm not!" said Bob-Along. "It's Mr. Knobbly that's dishonest! You ask him how many crackers he's *not* put toys into! You try on one of his funny hats and see how the elastic snaps at once. Well, he may trick *you*—but he's not going to trick *me*!"

"Wait!" said Mr. Popple. "Come down to Knobbly's with me. I'll soon get your money for you!" And away he went with Bob-Along grinning beside him. What a shock Mr. Knobbly had when they walked into his shop. Mr. Popple shook all the crackers and found that nineteen of them were empty! He tried on three funny hats and each time the elastic snapped almost at once.

"Ha! And you wouldn't pay a fair wage to this good worker here!" shouted Mr. Popple. "Wait till I get my wand! I'll wish you away to the darkest cave in the mountains, you dishonest brownie!"

But Mr. Knobbly didn't wait. He took to his heels and fled, and never came back again. And Bob-Along quickly put strong elastic on to the hats and filled the empty crackers, and blew up the flat balloons—*and* went to the party too!

And who do you suppose has Knobbly's shop now? Yes, little Bob-Along, with his merry face and honest ways. Well, he deserves to have it, doesn't he!

The Little White Hen

ONCE a little white hen came wandering into the garden belonging to Snip and Snap the brownies. They were surprised and pleased.

"We'll try and find out where she belongs, and if we can't, we'll keep her for our own," said Snip.

So they asked everyone in the village if they knew whose the little white hen was, but nobody knew at all. So Snip and Snap kept her.

"We'll make her a dear little hen-house out of a wooden box," said Snip.

"And we'll put a little nest of hay in one corner for her to lay her eggs in," said Snap.

"And she shall be called Snowball," said Snip.

"That's a silly name for a hen," said Snap. "That's a cat's name."

"Well, call her White-Feathers then," said Snip.

So they called her White-Feathers, and threw down some corn for her to peck up. She ran to it with loud clucks and pecked it all up in a few minutes. Then she went into the box that Snip and Snap had set ready for her, and sat down on the hay in the corner.

"She's going to lay us an egg," said Snip, delighted.

"I shall have it for my breakfast," said Snap.

"No, you won't!" said Snip at once. "I shall have it for my tea."

"Cluck!" said the hen, and got off the nest. And there, in the middle of the hay, was the prettiest brown egg you ever saw. The brownies stared in delight. Snip stooped

down and got out the egg. It was smooth and warm in his hand.

" Thank you, White-Feathers," he said. "Thank you very much ! "

The brownies looked at the brown egg with joy. This was marvellous !

" Snip, this hen will bring us luck ! " said Snap. " If she lays an egg every single day, we can sell some of them. We could sell three of them at threepence each. That's ninepence a week. We could have the other four for ourselves. What shall we do with ninepence a week ? "

" Save it up and buy a little pig ! " said Snip. " I've always wanted a pig. They look so round and fat and comfortable. Yes—we'll buy a pig."

" And the pig will grow simply enormous, and we'll sell it and get a *lot* of money ! " said Snap. " My goodness, we shall be rich! We might get a whole pound for the pig. What shall we call the pig, Snip?"

"We'll call him Roundy," said Snip. "That's a good name for a pig. Well, what shall we do with the pound that we get for the pig?"

"We'll buy a cow, and we'll call her Mooey," said Snap. "And we can milk her each day and sell the milk. Snip, we shall soon be rich! Fancy that! What shall we do with all our money? We'll have bags and bags of it."

"Well, we'll buy ourselves new suits of silver and gold," said Snip.

"And we'll build a new house with a hundred windows and sixty chimneys," said Snap.

"And I'll have a horse and carriage that will go trit-trot, trit-trot all through the town, and make people stare like anything," said Snip.

"Oh, no!" said Snap at once. "Not a horse and carriage, Snip. That's very old-fashioned. We'll have a bright-red

motor-car with yellow wheels, and a horn that goes honk-a-honk-a-honk. Then everyone will jump quickly out of the way ! "

" Everybody has a motor car," said Snip. "I want to be different. I want a horse and carriage. And my horse shall be called Clippitty-Clop. And when it goes along its hoofs will say its name all the time—clippity-clop, clippity-clop."

" *No*, Snip," said Snap. " I tell you we'll have a motor car. Don't you want to go honk-a-honk-honk and make everyone rush out of the way ? "

" No, I don't," said Snip. " And, anyway, I can make people get out of my way with a horse and carriage, can't I ? I can whip my horse and make him go like the wind. And what is more, Snap, if I see *you* coming along I'll gallop him straight at you and make you jump on to the pavement ! "

" Oh, *will* you? " cried Snap. " Well, let me tell you this, Snip—when I've got my motor car I'll drive round the town

till I see you coming, and I'll honk my horn so loudly that you'll drop all your shopping, and then I'll drive my red motor car at you, and run you over—bang, bump!"

"You horrid, unkind thing!" said Snip in a trembling voice. "If you do that, I'll gallop right over you with my horse and tell him to kick you away to the moon."

"You won't, you won't!" cried Snap. "Look—here I come at you with my motor car—look out!"

The angry little brownie pretended that he was in a car, and he rushed at Snip, making a noise like a motor-horn—honk-honk HONK!

"Well, you look out too, then!" shouted Snip, and he pretended he was riding on a horse. He galloped at Snap, and the two brownies bumped together so hard that all their breath went. Snip fell over, bang!

He jumped up in a great rage. He still had the egg in his

hand and he thought it was a stone. He threw it hard at Snap. But he missed him—and the egg sailed through the air and flew straight at White-Feathers the hen, who was listening to the quarrel, quite frightened.

Blip! The egg hit her hard on the beak. It broke, and the yellow yolk streamed out and fell to the ground. White-Feathers gave an angry cluck.

"Cluck, cluck, cluck! If that's the way you treat my nice brown egg, I won't stay with you! Cluck, cluck! Good-bye!"

And she spread her pretty white wings and flew right over the fence. Off she went, flapping and running, and the two brownies stared after her in great surprise.

" Come back, White-Feathers, come back ! " called Snip, crying big tears down his cheeks.

But she didn't come back. Goodness knows where she went !

" There goes our hen—and Roundy, our nice little pig—and Mooey, our dear cow—and our horse and carriage and bright-red motor car with yellow wheels," wept Snap.

" And we've lost that nice little brown egg too," sobbed Snip. " I'm sorry I was so silly, Snap. Do forgive me."

" I will, because I'm sorry too," said Snap. " Oh, why did we spoil our piece of good luck ? Never mind, Snip—next time a little white hen comes into our garden, we won't quarrel and lose her ! "

But so far no white hen has come again. Isn't it a pity ? It just shows how silly it is to quarrel, Snip and Snap !

Oh, Sammy!

PEOPLE were always saying " Oh, Sammy ! " to Sammy. He did such silly things. Once he put on his dirty jersey *and* his clean jersey too, and his mother hunted all the morning for the dirty one because she wanted to wash it. But Sammy was wearing them both at school, feeling very hot and wondering why.

Once his teacher told him to sharpen his pencils, and Sammy took the pens instead, and sharpened all the wooden ends. And another time the teacher told him to fill up the flower-vases with water from the jug, and Sammy took the milk-jug by mistake and put milk into all the jars and bowls.

He really was a silly little boy, and it was no wonder that people kept saying "Oh, Sammy!" to him. They said it in surprise. They said it in rage. They said it in sadness, to think that a boy should be so silly.

But Sammy didn't bother much. He just looked at everyone and said "Sorry!" But he never seemed to try and do better.

Now one day his teacher planned a treat for all his boys. "We will take the day off to-morrow," said kind Mr. Brown. "The weather is so fine now. Bring sandwiches to school with you, a bathing costume and a towel, and sixpence for bus fares and a drink."

"Ooooh!" said all the boys, excited. Sammy especially was pleased, because he was a fine swimmer, and there was nothing he liked more than bathing and swimming.

"Take your homework down now," said Mr. Brown. "I shall, of course, expect you to do a good deal of work to-night at home, to make up for missing school to-morrow. But I am sure you won't mind that."

" Of course not, sir ! " said all the boys, and they began to write down what they were to do for homework. They had to do sums, which they wrote down carefully, copying them from the blackboard. They had to learn a list of spelling words. They had to learn a long piece of poetry, which they also copied down from the blackboard.

" Everything down in your note-books ? " asked Mr. Brown. " That's good. Now please remember—any boy who shirks his homework to-night will not go with us to-morrow. I expect good work from you in return for a treat."

" Of course, sir," said the boys, and they all made up their minds to do their very, very best.

" Does anyone pass by old Mr. Jones' house ? " asked Mr. Brown, as the boys began to pack up their things. " I want someone to take a note to him."

" I pass his house, sir," said Sammy. " I'm the only one that goes that way. All the others go the opposite way ; I'll take it, sir."

" Thank you, Sammy," said Mr. Brown. Sammy took the note and put it into his pocket. Off he went home, his homework note-book in his other pocket. Sammy meant to do some marvellous work that night just to show Mr. Brown how glad he was to have a day's holiday the next morning.

Sammy came to old Mr. Jones' house. He rang the bell. Nobody came—but in the hall a little dog barked and growled. " Bother ! " said Sammy. " I believe Mr. Jones is out." He knocked loudly and the little dog inside nearly went mad with rage.

" Bark and growl all you like," said Sammy. " I've only come to bring a note to your master."

Nobody answered the door. There was nobody in but the dog. " Well, I must put the note through the letter-box, that's all," said Sammy, and slipped his hand into the wide brass letter-box.

Then he went home. He had tea and told his mother all about the treat for the next day. "I'm going to do a good evening's work," he said, and settled down at the table. He put his hand into his pocket to take out his homework note-book—but instead he pulled out the note for Mr. Jones!

How very extraordinary! What was the note doing in his pocket? Surely he had put it into Mr. Jones' letter-box! Quickly Sammy hunted through his pockets for his homework note-book. It wasn't there!

"Mother! Oh, Mother! I've posted my note-book in Mr. Jones' letter-box, instead of the letter that Mr. Brown gave me!" wailed Sammy. "Mother, what am I to do? I must do my homework to-night. It's the treat to-morrow."

"Oh, Sammy!" said his mother, as she had said a thousand times before. "Oh, Sammy!" She stared at him in dismay.

Why *did* Sammy do these silly things? " Well," she said, " you must go back to Mr. Jones' house and see if he's home yet, that's all. Then you can give him the note and ask him for your note-book."

" Yes, I'll do that," said Sammy, cheering up. " I expect he's back by now." He put on his cap and raced off to Mr. Jones' house. He rang and he knocked, but the only answer he got was the barking of the furious little dog inside.

" Oh dear—he's not back yet," said poor Sammy. " Well— I must wait, that's all."

So he sat down on the front doorstep and waited for Mr. Jones to come home. He waited and he waited. The little dog barked and growled. Mr. Jones didn't come.

Six o'clock struck from the church tower. Seven o'clock struck. This was dreadful! Sammy was cold and tired and worried. Oh, Mr. Jones, do come!

Then, at almost half-past seven, old Mr. Jones came walking

briskly up the street. He was most surprised to see Sammy on his doorstep.

"Please, Mr. Jones," said Sammy, "Mr. Brown gave me a note for you—but by mistake I put my homework note-book into your letter-box. So I've been waiting here for you to come home so that you could open your door and give it to me."

"Oh, Sammy! Whatever will you do next?" said Mr. Jones, with a laugh. He opened the door, and Sammy stooped to get his note-book. The little dog stared at him, barking. "Down, Tinker, down!" said Mr. Jones, sternly.

Then what a shock there was for poor Sammy! Tinker had torn his note-book into rags! Every page had been nibbled and chewed. Poor Sammy couldn't read what he had written there that morning. His note-book was nothing but scraps of torn paper.

He burst into tears and ran home. It was dark now, and his mother was worried about him. He ran into the house and sobbed out the tale of the torn note-book. " Mother ! I must go round to Tim's or Peter's, and copy down from their note-book what my homework is," he said.

" It's too late to do that now," said his mother. " You ought to have thought of that before. I will write a note to explain to Mr. Brown to-morrow."

She did—but when Mr. Brown read it, he shook his head and frowned. " I'm sorry about this, Sammy, " he said. " But I can't excuse your homework to-day—you see, it was because of your own silliness that it isn't done. Silliness is just as bad as carelessness or laziness. Just as bad. So I'm afraid, my boy, you must stay here at school and do your homework, while we go off for our picnic."

" Oh, Mr. Brown ! " said Sammy, nearly in tears.

" Oh, Sammy ! " said Mr. Brown. " Now sit down and begin, Sammy. When you have finished, catch the bus and join us—but finish all your work first. And Sammy—*don't* let your silliness rob you of any treat in the future ! "

" I won't, I won't," said Sammy, sitting down and looking at the blackboard. " I know it's not you that's punishing me, Mr. Brown. I know it's my own silly self. I couldn't stop *you* punishing me, if you wanted to—but I *can* stop myself, can't I ? "

" Yes—if you want to hard enough ! " said Mr. Brown. " Well—good-bye ! Perhaps we shall see you later in the day ! "

He did—because Sammy did two hours' hard work, and then caught the bus. He missed a good deal of the treat, but he did have some of it ! And do you know, Sammy is quite glad he *had* to miss some of it. Because, you see, it gave him a shock, and taught him a lesson.

" And now," says Sammy, " I shan't be silly any more ! "

Who Was The Thief?

"WHO'S been taking Daddy's walnuts off the sideboard?" asked Mummy.

"I haven't!" said Dick.

"And I haven't either!" said Alice. "You *know* we wouldn't, Mummy!"

"Well, somebody has," said Mummy. "And I know where they've been taken to."

"Where?" asked both children.

"Out into the garden, by your swing," said Mummy, looking very solemn. "Now you know you can have walnuts if you ask—but not unless. I saw the broken shells of walnuts all round your swing."

"You mean—you thought *we'd* taken them there and cracked them and left the shells all about?" said Alice. "Oh, Mummy, we didn't. Truly we didn't. Don't you believe us?"

Mummy looked at both children, puzzled and worried. "Very well. I do believe you," she said. "But it's very queer. There's nobody but us in the house, and Mrs. Toms, who comes to do the cleaning. And she never comes in here."

Mummy went out of the room, still looking puzzled. The children looked at one another.

"As if we'd take anything belonging to Daddy!" said Dick fiercely.

"Or belonging to *any*one!" said Alice. "Mummy ought to know she can trust us—but all the same, it's queer about the nuts, isn't it? *Some*body must be taking them—and going out into the garden with them! Do you suppose it's Jock, that naughty little boy next door?"

"It might be," said Dick. "Though he always throws back our balls when they go over. He chases our cat, though, and he's very rude to his mother. I've heard him."

"Well, perhaps it's Jock," said Alice. "I wish we could catch him. Dick—shall we hide in here and see if anyone creeps in?"

"Yes! That's about the only way we'll find out who the thief is," said Dick. "But first let's go to our swing and see how many nutshells are there."

So they went to their swing—and sure enough, as Mummy had said, there were many walnut shells scattered about, all round the swing.

"It looks as if the thief came and sat on the swing while he cracked and ate the nuts," said Dick. "It *must* be the boy next door!"

They felt so cross about it that when Jock called to them and asked them to come and play with him they said no, they didn't want to, and walked indoors. He was very surprised.

" Let's count the walnuts, then we shall know when any are gone," said Dick, so they counted them. " Only fifteen," he said. " Well, we'll just go and do the shopping for Mummy, then when we come back we'll hide here and watch to see if the thief comes."

They went off with the shopping basket, and came back with it quite full. Mummy was pleased. " Now you can go and help yourselves to an apple each," she said. " The two rosiest ones in the dish ! "

They went into the dining-room and chose two apples. " Let's just count the walnuts," said Dick, and he counted them. He looked at Alice, surprised.

" Only *fourteen* now ! One's gone—but only one. Well then, the thief must have come while we were out shopping ! Alice, let's crouch down behind the big couch and wait there to watch. We can eat our apples too."

So they squeezed behind the big couch and sat there, nibbling their juicy apples. " Mine's lovely and sweet!" whispered Alice.

" So's mine," said Dick. " But I'm not very comfortable here, are you ? Alice, if you hear anything give me a nudge."

They sat and munched their apples, and listened carefully in case anyone came creeping in at the door that led into the

garden. But they didn't hear anyone at all. Then suddenly
Alice nudged Dick and made him jump. He listened hard.

"Someone at the dish!" whispered Alice. And sure
enough Dick could hear the tiny rattle of nuts on the dish.
Who was it there? He waited to hear the somebody go creeping back to the garden door, but he heard nothing. So he popped up his head from behind the couch and shouted loudly :

"WHO'S THERE?"

And there was nobody there at all! Dick was so surprised.
He scrambled out and went to the dish. He counted the nuts.
"Alice!" he said. "There are only *thirteen* walnuts now!
Another one's gone. While we were hiding too! How
was it we never heard them going in and out of the door?"

"I don't know. They must have been very very quiet," said
Alice. "Let's hide again. He may come back. If it's Jock I
vote we pounce on him and yell for Mummy." They hid again
and finished their apples. And then Alice gave Dick a nudge
as she heard a little sound on the sideboard. The thief was there
again.

Both children rose up from behind the couch at once,
shouting, "THIEF! THIEF!"

Something seemed to fly across the room like lightning, something small and red. It disappeared out of the garden door. Dick clutched Alice.

" What was it ? Did you see ? It seemed to *fly* ! Alice, it couldn't have been a goblin or something, could it ? "

Alice began to laugh. She sat down on the couch and laughed and laughed. Dick was cross and shook her. " Alice ! What was it ? Tell me, was it the thief ? "

" Yes," said Alice, still smiling. " Yes, it was. Oh dear— to think we never guessed ! We even know the thief's name, Dick."

" Well, *tell* me ! " said Dick, getting quite angry.

" It was Frisky—the little red squirrel who lives in the woods at the bottom of our garden ! " said Alice. " You know how he loves the hazel-nuts. Well, I expect he came peeping in here and saw the walnuts and thought he would try those too. And I daresay if we look out of the window we'll see him sitting on our swing and cracking one ! "

" Well ! We never thought of him ! " said Dick. " Oh, I *am* glad it's Frisky. Let's tell Mother ! "

So they did and she laughed too. Alice and Dick went to see if they could find Frisky in the garden, but he was gone. They heard Jock next door, whistling.

"Let's ask him in to play with us," said Dick. "I feel ashamed that we thought he was the thief!"

So they called to Jock and he came over the wall. "I began to think you didn't like me!" he said.

They played Red Indians, in the wood—and a little red squirrel sat watching, cracking a big round nut. Yes—you're right—it was Frisky and his stolen walnut!

The Quiet Kite

WHEN the kite came to live in the nursery the other toys couldn't understand it at all.

"It's not a doll," said the red-haired doll.

"It's not a bear," said the teddy.

"It's not an engine," said the train.

"It's a silly sort of toy," said the rocking-horse, looking into the toy-cupboard, where the kite lay quiet and still. "It has no legs, so it can't run about with us. It can't even roll, like the balls!"

"It has a tail, but doesn't wag it," said the pink dog, who was very proud of his tail because it wagged to and fro when he was wound up.

Everyone looked at the kite's long tail. It was made of screwed-up bits of paper tied to a long string.

The kite suddenly spoke, in a kind of windy, wheezy voice.

"I daren't move my tail in case it gets tangled up," it said. "It takes such a time to untangle it, you know."

"Oh, the kite can talk!" cried the red-haired doll. "Do come out and play, Kite."

"No, thank you," said the kite. "As the rocking-horse said, I have no legs, so I can't walk. I prefer to stay here quietly."

And there the kite stayed, and wouldn't move. The toys laughed at it. They pulled its tail. They unwound its string and got it all muddled. The kite was very upset.

"Don't do that," it said. "I may want that string some day."

"Pooh! What for?" cried the teddy-bear. "What do

kites do ? Nothing, so far as I can see ! Except just lie about in the cupboard and get lazier and lazier."

And the bad bear tangled the string up even more. The kite was very unhappy about it, for it had no arms or legs to undo the knots.

But the little white ostrich out of the Noah's Ark was very kind. She came up to undo the tangle. And very soon the kite and the ostrich made friends.

" Where's the other ostrich ? " asked the kite. " I thought there were two of every animal and bird in the ark."

" Well, there *were* two ostriches," said the little white ostrich, " but the other one got trodden on and broken. So now there is only me. And I am often lonely because I am by myself. The other animals are in pairs."

" Don't be lonely," said the kite. " Come and talk to me when you feel sad."

So after that the ostrich and the kite often talked together, though everyone else laughed at them.

" What you can see in that silly, quiet kite I really can't imagine ! " said the teddy-bear to the ostrich.

" And what the kite can see in that stupid wooden little ostrich puzzles *me* ! " said the red-haired doll, tossing her thick curls. Now one day the wind got up out-of-doors and roared away into the sky, blowing the clouds along and twisting the chimney smoke like ribbon. And into the nursery ran John, to whom all the toys belonged.

" Where's my kite ? Where's my kite ? " he cried. " It's just the day for a kite ! Kite, kite, where are you ? "

He pulled the kite out of the cupboard and shook out its tail. " Come along ! " he cried. " It's just the day for a fine kite like you ! "

His sister Winnie came into the nursery too. " Oh, have

you found your kite ? " she said. " Good, John. I'll bring all the toys into the garden to watch ! "

So she picked up the toys, little white ostrich and all, and followed her brother into the garden. The toys were most surprised. What was all this fuss about the kite ? Why was this windy day just the day for it ? They simply couldn't imagine !

Winnie set the toys down on the grass. John began to unwind a little of the string that was tied to the kite. He shook out the lovely long tail.

The wind caught hold of the kite and pulled at it in delight. John threw it up into the air. At once it rose high, and higher still as John let out more and more string. It quivered and shook like a live thing. Its lovely tail swung below it, twisting and shaking. It was marvellous !

" Oh, Winnie ! Doesn't the kite fly beautifully ? " cried John, pleased. " It's the best kite in the world ! Oh, look, it's pulling so hard at my hand that it feels like a horse wanting to gallop away ! "

" Well, hold on tight," said Winnie. " It would be dreadful if you let go and it flew away by itself ! Hold on tight ! "

All the toys watched in amazement. Could this really be the poor quiet kite they had so often laughed at ? The kite that had no legs and couldn't play with them ? The kite whom they had teased and tangled ? They couldn't believe it ! It was flying higher and higher in the air, sometimes dipping down in great circles, sometimes flapping its tail in glee. It was lovely to watch.

" Would you believe that the quiet old kite could fly like that ? " said the red-haired doll.

" *I* couldn't fly up in the air," said the teddy.

" It's much, much cleverer than we are," said the train.

The little white ostrich was proud of her fine friend. She

watched out of her black eyes and wondered if the kite would bump into the big white clouds that raced along so fast.

At last the wind dropped and the kite swooped down. It lay on the grass quite quiet. John heard his mother calling and turned to Winnie. " Come on—that's Mother. She has some biscuits for us ! "

The children raced indoors. Soon the wind began to blow again and the kite lifted itself a little from the grass. " Ostrich," it called, " climb on to my tail ! I'll give you a fly ! You are a nice little bird and you ought to try how lovely it is to fly through the air ! "

" Ostriches don't fly. They only run ! " called the teddy-bear, jealously. He would so very much have loved to climb on to the end of the kite's tail himself.

" *This* ostrich is going to fly ! " said the little white ostrich, and she settled herself on the very end of the kite's tail. There came a great gust of wind and the kite rose up joyously. It flew up into the air, dragging its long tail behind it. And on the end flew the little white ostrich half delighted, half frightened, but enjoying herself thoroughly.

" The kite will fly away and John will be cross," said the teddy. But the kite didn't, because John had been wise enough to tie the end of its string to a post. So when the kite rose very high it had to stay there, because the string was tied fast to the post and the kite couldn't get away.

Soon John and Winnie came out with their biscuits. "Look!" cried John. " My kite is flying itself. Isn't it clever ! "

When he pulled down the kite to put it away, John had such a surprise. He called to Winnie.

" Winnie! Look! Your little white ostrich has been for a fly on the tail of the kite! Isn't that queer? "

When the kite was put away in the toy-cupboard that night, the toys came up to it. They felt ashamed.

" Kite, you were marvellous to-day," said the red-haired doll.

" Kite, I'm sorry I tangled your string," said the bear. " I didn't know how important your string was to you."

" It's quite all right," said the kite generously. "I know I'm quiet and dull when I'm lying here doing nothing, but I'm a different fellow, I can tell you, when I'm up in the air! "

" Give the others a ride on your tail next time," said the little white ostrich, who was pleased to find that the toys were being nice to her friend.

" I will! " said the kite. And it'll keep its word, no doubt about that. I'd love to see the red-haired doll swinging on the end of its tail, wouldn't you?

Beware of the Bull!

"I SAY! Look at all those red apples on that tree!" said Tom, looking over Farmer Corn's hedge.

Harry looked all round. "Let's get over the hedge and get some. There's nobody to see us!"

"The hedge is too tall here to get over," said Tom. "Anyway, we mustn't get other people's apples. That's stealing."

But Harry was running along the hedge, trying to find a way to get over. He suddenly came to a gate. "Look here! This is easy! We can get over the gate."

"No, don't," said Tom, and he pointed to a big notice nearby. "Look—it says 'BEWARE OF THE BULL!'"

Harry peered over the gate into the field where the apple tree grew. There was no bull to be seen. He laughed.

"Pooh! That notice is put there just to scare away anyone who wants those apples!" he said. "There's no bull. I'm going over the gate, and up that tree! I'll fill my pockets with apples. Come on, Tom."

"No," said Tom. "It really is stealing. If the farmer sees you he will be awfully angry."

"I'll be up the tree! *He* won't see me!" said Harry and climbed over the gate. He ran to the tree and was up in a trice. He began to fill his pockets with apples.

Tom heard someone coming down the lane. It was Farmer Corn—and with him was the bull! Farmer Corn had been walking it to another farm and back. Now he was bringing it to its field again!

Tom slipped away, frightened. The farmer opened the gate and sent the bull in. It bellowed loudly, and stared round with fierce red eyes. The farmer shut the gate. He walked away, whistling.

Harry heard the gate click and looked between the leaves of the tree he was in. He saw the bull coming across the field! His heart stood still with fright.

The bull! That hadn't been a notice to scare away apple-thieves—it had been an honest warning!

" What am I to do ? " thought Harry, scared. " I daren't get down and run for it—the bull will see me and toss me. And I daren't call out to the farmer, because he will know I've been stealing his apples."

The bull bellowed again. Harry felt very much afraid. Then he thought of Tom—of course, Tom would help him! " Tom ! " he yelled. " Tom ! "

Tom appeared at the gate, also looking scared. " Hey ! " called Harry. " Aren't you going to help me ? Can't you take the bull's attention whilst I get down and run ? "

" All right," said Tom, and began to pretend to climb over the gate. The bull saw him, bellowed and ran to the gate at

D

once. Harry shinned down the tree and ran to the hedge in the opposite direction ! But alas for him—there was barbed wire in the hedge there, and before he was safely through, his coat was torn to ribbons ! Whatever would his mother say ?

She said a great deal. " You bad boy ! Look at your coat ! Whatever have you been doing ? You will have to pay for the mending of that yourself, and it will take you two months of your pocket-money ! "

" Oh, Mother ! " wailed Harry.

" If only you hadn't run off this afternoon without telling me where you were going, you would have had a nice treat ! " said his mother. " Mrs. Corn, the farmer's wife, came along to ask if you and Tom would help with the apple-picking this afternoon—and in return you could take a basketful of apples each ! "

Well ! Think of that ! They could have had the apples, as many as they wanted, and enjoyed themselves too. " I told you it was wrong, I told you ! " said Tom. " It jolly well serves you right ! "

And I rather think it did, don't you ?

What a Thing to Happen!

"G RANNY is going to have a little nap," Mummy said to Peter. "So don't make too much noise playing round her in the garden, will you!"

"No, I'll be very quiet," said Peter. "I'll read my new book." So he sat down with his book. Granny smiled at him from her deck-chair and then shut her eyes.

Peter read to the end of his book, and then he looked at Granny. If only she was awake he could ride his new little bicycle round the garden. What a pity it hadn't a bell! He did so want a nice, jingly bell, but Mummy had said he must save up for it.

He went over to look at his bicycle. It was still so new that he hadn't got used to it yet.

And then suddenly something most peculiar happened ! A little man ran into the garden, wearing a long, pointed hat and pointed shoes. He had pointed ears too, and bright green eyes, and looked very like someone out of a fairy-tale book !

He saw Peter by his bicycle, looking at him in astonishment. He ran to him and called out loudly, " Will you lend me your bicycle, please ? "

" Sh ! My Granny's asleep," said Peter. " Why do you want my bicycle ? It's almost a new one."

" Well, I want to go after someone who's stolen my black cat," said the little man. " It's a magic cat that helps me with my spells. And Sly-One came by this morning, saw my cat on the windowsill and ran off with him. I really must get him back."

Peter couldn't help feeling very astonished. " I can't let you borrow my bicycle," he said, " unless of course I go with you. You can ride it and I'll stand on the step behind."

"Right," said the little man, and leapt on the bicycle. Peter just had time to stand on the step and put his hands on the little man's shoulders—then away they went at top speed down the garden path!

"Look out for the hedge!" gasped Peter, but the little man took no notice at all—and to Peter's amazement the bicycle jumped right over the hedge as easily as anything! Really, this was all very very surprising!

"There he is, see—the fellow who stole my cat!" cried the little man suddenly, and far away in front Peter saw someone else, hurrying along, carrying something black under his arm. On they went and on, and came to a little market-place which Peter had never seen before in any of his walks.

All kinds of queer folk were there, and the little man nearly knocked some of them down. "Where's your bicycle bell?" he shouted to Peter. "I can't find it. I simply must ring it to make people get out of my way or I shall lose my cat!"

" There isn't a bell," said Peter. " I'm so sorry. I'm saving
up for one, you see ! "

" A bicycle without a bell ! " said the little man, quite
crossly. " Never heard of such a thing ! Get out of the way,
you ! Hey, there, make way, will you ! "

At last they were out of the market-place and riding through
a wood—and here the little rabbits kept popping across the
path and the little man grew angrier than ever.

" How can I make them get out of the way without a bell ! "
he cried. " Wait—I must make one by magic." And he leapt off

the bicycle, drew a circle in the dust with a twig, muttered some very magic words—and there, in the middle of the circle, appeared a bright, shining new bicycle bell. It really was most remarkable.

The little man fastened it to the bicycle handle, and away they went again, this time with the bell ringing all the time— jingle-jingle-jingle-jingle, r-r-r-ring, r-r-r-ing !

" Ah—there's Sly-One ! We've got him now ! " said the little man, and to Peter's horror he rode straight into the back of the running man and knocked him flat !

He dropped the big black cat he was carrying and the cat at
once jumped on to the little man's shoulder and began purring
loudly.

"Get up!" said the little man to the thief, who was lying
on the ground. "Get up! I'm taking you to the nearest
policeman. How DARE you steal a magic cat!"

"Do you want my bicycle any more?" asked Peter. "It
really won't take three of us."

" No, thank you. No, I don't," said the little man. " You ride home now. Many thanks for helping me to rescue my dear old cat."

" But I don't know my way home," said Peter, in alarm.

" Never mind ! The bicycle does," said the little man. " Get on, and I'll give you a push, and it won't stop till you ride in at your garden gate. Go on now—I promise you it will take you home ! "

Peter mounted the saddle and the little man gave him a push, and off went the bicycle at top speed. It certainly did seem to know the way ! It went through the wood and came to the market. It went through that and into the fields, and Peter wondered how it could possibly know the way when *he* didn't !

He rang the bell loudly whenever he came across any rabbits, because he didn't want to hurt one, and it was plain that the bicycle didn't mean to stop until it was safely home. It even seemed to work its pedals itself, and they flew up and down, with Peter's feet doing their best to keep up with them.

He rode into his own garden, the bicycle having done a most surprising leap over the hedge again. Really, Peter was quite glad to be able to get off and lean it against a tree ! He looked at Granny—and she was awake !

" Wherever have you been on your bicycle, dear ? " she said, and Peter told her. How Granny laughed.

"Oh, what a story!" she said. "Surely you can't expect me to believe a tale like *that*, Peter! You've been asleep and dreaming! As for your bicycle ringing its bell at rabbits and things—why, you know very well it hasn't one. You're saving up for one!"

"Well—it's very queer, Granny, but my bicycle still has the bell the little man made for it!" said Peter, and he went to his bicycle and rang the bell— jingle-jingle-jingle-jing, rrrrring, rrrrring!

And Peter *still* has the very same bell—isn't that queer! So it couldn't have been a dream, could it, as Granny thought? What a thing to happen on a quiet summer's afternoon!

Hide and Seek

Someone is playing along the lane,
Calling out "Cuckoo!" again and again,
Who is it playing at hide-and-seek?
I never can see, though I go and peek.

Is it Harry or Hilda or Mary Ann?
I try to spy but I never can.
Is it Ellen or Mollie—or can it be
A mischievous elf making fun of me?

"Cuckoo! Cuckoo!" There it goes again!
There *is* someone hiding along our lane—
I've found him now—
And what *do* you suppose,
It's the *cuckoo*—the cuckoo that everyone knows!

You Simply Never Know!

"Buck up, Sally—we'll miss our train home from school!" called Benny. "Do hurry!"

"I'm just telling Jane what we have to do for home-work!" shouted Sally. "She's torn up her notes by mistake. Shan't be a minute."

But she was more than a minute helping Jane, and she and Benny had to run at top speed to the station.

When they got there, they saw the train at the platform—and just as they ran on, it began to pull out. Ch-ch-ch-ch-CH!

"Wait, wait!" shouted Benny. But it didn't wait, of course, and the porter pulled them back as they ran towards it.

"Now, now—don't try anything silly," he said. "You'll have to wait for the next one."

"But it doesn't come for an hour," said Sally in despair. "And we were going to the circus this evening. We shall be much too late."

"Well, you children dawdle along so," said the porter, who was tired of seeing children race on to the platform at the very last minute.

"I *didn't* dawdle!" said Sally. "I had to stay and help a friend." But the porter wasn't listening. She turned to Benny. "What shall we do? Walk home?"

"Have to, I suppose," said Benny gloomily. "Well, that's what comes of doing a kind deed—we lost our train and our chance of going to the circus. *I* shan't do any kind deeds for some time!"

"I feel like that too," said Sally, trying not to cry. It really did seem too bad to have to walk home, just because she had stayed to tell Jane what the homework was.

They set off. It was such a long, long way to walk—almost five miles! They were hungry too, and what a long time they would have to wait for their tea!

"We'll cut across the fields," said Benny. "It's shorter than by the road, and nicer. Cheer up, Sally. We may be able to go to the circus another time."

"But Daddy's got the tickets for this evening," said Sally. "They'll be wasted! It begins at half-past five in the big field over the hill. I'm sure Daddy won't buy another set of tickets. And I did so want to see that elephant that can play tennis!"

They plodded on over the fields. Sally felt tired after a bit. She had played basket-ball that afternoon and really didn't want to have to walk so far now. On and on they went and then Benny looked at his watch.

"We've come a mile," he said, "and we've taken twenty

minutes. Not bad, considering it's over rough fields. Hallo—
what's that noise ? "

" Only an aeroplane," said Sally, gloomily, not even looking
up. But soon the sound was so very loud that she did look up,
half alarmed.

" Gracious ! It's coming down ! " she said. " Oh look,
Ben—it's landing in this very field. I wonder if anything has
gone wrong with it."

A man got out of the plane and shouted to them. They ran
to him as fast as they could.

" I say—can you tell me if I'm anywhere near Hooley Hill ?"
he said. " I'm taking a cage of monkeys to the circus in the
field near there, and I can't seem to find it."

" Oh ! Are you really ? " said Sally, surprised. " Yes,
you're not far from Hooley Hill—about five miles, I suppose.
The circus is just the other side, in an enormous field. You
can't fail to see it."

" We were going there ourselves tonight," said Benny.
" But we missed our train and now we've got to walk home—
five miles, too ! Otherwise we'd have been at the circus and
seen your monkeys. Where are they ? "

" In that cage, look," said the man, and the children peeped
into the plane and saw three small monkeys huddled together
in a cage, looking rather scared.

" They don't like flying very much," said the man. " I'm
sorry you're not coming to the circus. What a long way you've
got to walk ! My uncle owns the circus, and if you had been
able to come I could have taken you behind the scenes and
introduced you to the clowns and everything."

" Oh—how I would have loved that ! " said Sally. " I do
like your little monkeys. What do they do in the circus ? "

" One rides a tiny bicycle and the others draw a small cart
with a bigger monkey in it," said the man. " They love circus

life, and are always up to mischief. They just don't like flying though. Well, I must be off."

He got back into the pilot's seat, and the children watched him. But suddenly he shouted again to them. "I say—I've got an idea! Why don't you let me take you to the circus in this plane? I can easily take you two kids, you won't weigh much. How'd you like that?"

Sally and Benny stared at him, struck dumb. What! Go flying in a plane? They had never been up in the air in their lives, and how they longed to go! Whatever would everyone say at school tomorrow? Benny found his voice first. "Oh yes, yes, YES!" he shouted, and ran at top speed to the plane. "Come on, Sally, quick. Oh I say! I can't believe it!"

The pilot helped them both in, and the monkeys looked up and chattered to them. They wanted to get out and run about!

R-r-r-r-r-r ! R-R-R-R-RRRRRRRRR !

The aeroplane's engines started up, and the propellers swung round fast. The little plane shook from end to end, and Sally caught hold of Benny's arm, half excited, half afraid.

" Up we go ! " said the pilot, and up they went, over the fields, and over the farm-houses. " Oh, everything looks so very, very small ! " said Sally in amazement, looking down. " See Mr. Hoe's farm, Benny ? It looks like a toy one—and the cows look as small as the ones in our toy farm ! "

It was thrilling to be up so high. The two children loved it, but the monkeys didn't. They chattered in alarm and cuddled together even more tightly.

" Oh goodness—here's Hooley Hill already ! " said Benny in amazement. " All those miles—and it seems we were only flying for half a minute ! Are you going down now ? "

" Yes—there's a nice flat field beyond the circus," said the pilot. The children could see the circus tents below, looking very small—but growing larger as the plane circled gently down. " Look out for a bump," said the pilot. " Ah—there's my uncle watching for me."

BUMP ! They landed and taxied over the grass. A big

man ran over to them. " Got the monkeys, Sid ? " he asked. " Hallo—who are these kids ? "

" Oh, just two that told me the way," said the pilot, climbing out. " They'd better telephone to their home, Uncle, and say where they are. I brought them along in the plane to save them a long walk."

" The things you do," said his uncle. " Well, if the children want to telephone, there's a box down there in the lane."

" You go and telephone, kids," said the pilot, carrying out the cage of monkeys. " Then come back to me. I'll see that you and your parents get the best seats, and I'll take you behind as I promised, and introduce you to the clowns, and to Lotta, the girl who rides the horses, and to the performing dogs and all the rest."

Sally and Benny ran over the field to the lane, and soon saw the red telephone box. They rang up their mother and told her what had happened. She really could hardly believe it. " In an *aeroplane !* " she kept saying. " In an *aeroplane !* "

What a wonderful time the two children had that evening ! Their parents joined them in half an hour, and they were taken to the best seats in the ring. Sally and Benny were so excited that they could hardly wait for the circus to begin !

" And after the circus we'll be going behind the curtains to see the clowns and talk to them, and to meet Lotta the girl who rides the horses, and all the performing dogs, and Jumbo the elephant—it's too good to be true ! " said Sally.

And now the circus is just about to begin. The drums are rolling, the trumpets are blowing. The curtains are swinging apart, and in come the beautiful horses, and in comes the ringmaster too, with his great cracking whip, and his fine top hat. What a wonderful bow he gives !

And isn't it strange that if Sally hadn't stayed to help Jane with her homework she and Benny wouldn't have flown *or* gone to the circus ! Well, well—you simply never know !

The Squeaky Doll

THERE was once a tiny rubber doll, no bigger than your middle finger, who lived in Betsy-May's dolls' house. Betsy-May loved this doll because she could squeak. Whenever she was squeezed in her middle she said " Eee-eee," just like that.

But one day a dreadful thing happened to the rubber doll. Betsy-May took her out of the dolls' house to show her to Tommy, who had come to tea—and Tommy trod on her quite by accident.

And that killed the squeak in the poor little doll. She couldn't squeak any more at all. You can't think how sad she was, because, you see, it was the only voice she had.

There were three other dolls in the dolls' house—two tiny wooden ones and a little china one. They were very upset when the rubber doll lost her squeak.

"Let us put her to bed for a day," they said. "Maybe she will get her squeak back, if she rests."

So they put her to bed in one of the little beds in the dolls' bedroom, and looked after her well. But when she got up again, she still had no squeak, though all the dolls pressed her as hard as they could in the middle.

Betsy-May was just as sad as the dolls about it. She looked at the little rubber doll and squeezed her in the middle—but no squeak came.

"I don't like you so much now," said Betsy-May. "You don't seem right without a squeak."

Well, that made the rubber doll cry bitterly that night. It was dreadful not to be liked so much. After all, she couldn't help losing her squeak. The other dolls comforted her, and gave her a tiny sweet out of the toy sweet-shop.

Then they put her to bed again, and tucked her up well. They went down into the kitchen and talked about the poor rubber doll.

" It would be so lovely to hear her squeak again," said the china doll, lighting a tiny candle in a candlestick, for it was dark in the doll's kitchen.

And just at that very moment they heard a perfectly lovely squeak. " Eee-eee-eee ! " it went. " Eee-eee-eee ! "

" The rubber doll has got her squeak back ! " they cried, and they rushed upstairs. But no—how queer—the rubber doll was fast asleep and not squeaking at all. As the three dolls stood looking down on her, they heard the squeak again, " Eee-eee-eee ! "

And then somebody knocked quietly on the little knocker on the dolls' house front door. Down went the three dolls to see who it was.

Outside the door stood a tiny mouse. He twitched his fine whiskers and spoke humbly to the dolls.

"Oh, please, the golliwog told me you wanted a squeak, and I have a fine one. I am very, very hungry, so if you would give me something nice to eat, I will let you have my squeak." The dolls stared in delight. "Come in," said the china doll.

" I hope we *have* got something for you to eat. But I don't believe we have, you know."

The mouse went in. The dolls opened the little kitchen cupboard—but it was quite, quite empty. There was nothing to eat at all !

" Oh dear, what a pity," said the china doll. " It would have been marvellous to have got a new squeak for the rubber doll."

The baby mouse looked at the candle burning on the table. " Could I have that candle to eat ? " he asked. " It is made of tallow, and I like tallow."

" Good gracious ! Fancy wanting to eat a candle ! " cried the dolls. They blew it out at once, took it from the tiny candlestick, and gave it to the mouse. He asked them for a glass of water. When they gave it to him he squeaked into it about twenty times. Then he put his paw over the top of the glass and gave it to the china doll.

" Let the rubber doll drink this and her squeak will come back," he said. Then off he went out of the front door with his candle. What a treat for him !

The three dolls rushed upstairs and woke the surprised rubber doll. They made her drink the glass of water. Then they pressed her hard in the middle—and she said " EEEE-EEEE-EEEE ! " just like that. Wasn't she surprised !

" Oh, your squeak is back again ! " cried the china doll. " Won't Betsy-May be pleased ? "

Well, Betsy-May *was* pleased, of course—but she could never imagine where the little candle in the dolls' house had gone. *You* could tell her, couldn't you ?

Sly Squirrel Gets a Shock

SLY the Squirrel was a mean creature. He always got the best nuts for himself and the very nicest toadstools. He wouldn't let the nut-hatch bird have a single one of the nuts in the hazel wood where he lived, and if he caught the little dormouse taking one off the ground he would bound down and chatter at him angrily.

" They're my nuts, they're my nuts ! "

" They're not," said the dormouse. " You ask the hazel trees. They grow them for anyone."

" The squirrel is a meanie, the squirrel is a meanie," sang the nut-hatch, and whistled loud and long.

" Sly is his name and Sly is his nature ! " sang a little blue-tit who sometimes liked a nut himself.

" Nobody likes the squirrel, nobody likes the squirrel ! " squeaked the field-mouse, popping his head up from a hole under the roots of a pine-tree not far off.

The squirrel stared angrily round. It wasn't nice to have things shouted out about him like that. He was very much annoyed.

He bounded away to the top of a tree. It was late autumn, and there were many nuts hanging on the boughs. The squirrel picked one and bit it with his sharp teeth. He gnawed a hole in the nut to get at the sweet kernel.

But the kernel inside was not sweet. It was very bitter. The squirrel spat it out in disgust.

" A bad nut ! " he said. " There are such a lot this year. I wish the nut-hatch bird and the mice would get all the bad nuts, and I could get all the good ones. That would serve them right for being so mean to me."

As he sat and nibbled at a good nut, an idea came into his sly head.

" I know what I'll do ! I'll gather all the bad nuts I can find and put them into a pile, and I'll tell the nut-hatch and the mice I've picked them for a present for them ! Then they will be sorry they called me rude names, and will think I am a fine fellow. But what a shock they will get in the middle of the winter when they go to their store of nuts and find that they are all bad ! "

The mean little squirrel began to hunt for the bad nuts. He knew that they had little holes in them where the nut-grub had bitten its way out. He put them all together in a pile at the foot of one of the hazel trees.

"Look at Sly the Squirrel! He is piling up heaps of nuts for himself!" said the nut-hatch bird to the dormouse below.

The squirrel overheard him. "Those lovely nuts are not for myself," he said. "They are for you, and the dormouse and the field-mouse."

"I don't want them," said the dormouse. "I sleep all the winter through. I'm eating nuts myself now to get my body fat, so that I shall be able to sleep in comfort all the winter. It will soon be very cold weather."

The nut-hatch was surprised to hear that Sly the Squirrel had collected the nuts for the others, and not for himself.

" Thank you," he said. " I may visit the pile in the winter."

" I've plenty stored up for myself," said the field-mouse. " But maybe I'll find a few of your nuts useful, Sly. Thank you very much. The nut-hatch and I will cover them with leaves."

So he and the nut-hatch covered up the big pile of bad nuts with leaves.

Sly the Squirrel grinned to himself.

" What a shock they will get ! " he said.

Now that night the frost came. It came very suddenly indeed, before Sly the Squirrel expected it. He had been so busy collecting bad nuts for the others that he had had no time to collect good ones for himself. Usually he picked many nuts and hid them in corners and crannies, so that when he awoke on a warm day in the winter, and felt hungry, he would have plenty of nuts to find and eat.

It was terribly cold the next day. Sly woke up and looked out from his hole in the tree. " I'd better go out and find some

nuts to store away," he said sleepily. He put his nose out a bit farther, but the frost bit it and he drew it in again quickly.

"Oh! How cold! I'll sleep a bit longer!"

He slept for more than a month! When he did wake, he was dreadfully hungry. He leapt out of his hole into the winter sunshine. It was quite a warm day for winter time.

He looked about for nuts. The trees were quite bare. There were no leaves and no nuts. And then Sly remembered that he had not had time to store himself away any good nuts at all!

"Oh my! I didn't put away nuts as I usually do!" he said to himself. "Now what shall I do?"

He sat hugging his little empty tummy and then he saw the nut-hatch bird flying by, whistling.

"Hi, nut-hatch! Where are there any nuts?"

"Nowhere," said the bird. "The trees are bare."

Then Sly saw the little mouse. "Hi, field-mouse!" he called. "Have you any nuts stored up? Could you spare me a few?"

" No—I've only enough for myself and my family," said the mouse. " But have you forgotten that lovely pile over there— under those dead leaves ? "

Sly had forgotten all about them. " Where are they ? " he said eagerly.

" You can have them all," said the mouse. " They are just over there."

So Sly bounded over to the pile and brushed aside the leaves. He cracked the nuts hungrily.

But alas for the poor squirrel ! Every nut was bad, every single one ! The little mouse ran up and the nut-hatch flew down.

" What's the matter ? " they said, as they saw Sly throwing away one nut after another without eating it.

" Bad, bad, all bad ! " said Sly. " Why did you collect all bad nuts, you silly stupid things ? "

The nut-hatch whistled and the mouse squealed with laughter.

" Silly yourself ! It was *you* who collected that pile of nuts and gave them to *us*. Don't you remember ? "

And then at last Sly did remember ! Yes—he had picked all those bad nuts—with holes in—to give the nut-hatch and the field-mouse a really horrid shock.

The nut-hatch and the field-mouse went off laughing. " Serves you right ! " they cried.

So Sly the Squirrel had to go hungry all that winter, and if the little mouse hadn't been kind and given him a few of his own nuts, he would have starved. I don't think he'll play a trick like that again, do you ?

The Very Fat Conker

THE children were hunting for conkers under the big chestnut tree. It was a good conker year, and the tree had thrown down hundreds of its green, prickly cases, each with two, sometimes three, satiny-brown chestnuts inside. " Here's one with three ! " shouted Jim.

" Well, they'll be small ones then," called back Lennie. " I like to find a case with one enormous one and two tiddlers. I don't care about the tiddlers, but I do like the great big ones ! I got my fifty-three-er from a case with one big one and two little ones in it."

Lennie's fifty-three-er was a beautiful chestnut. It was very very big, very round and very smooth—and as hard as a brick ! He had bored a hole in it very carefully indeed, threaded through some string, and knotted one end. Then he swung it to and fro—yes, it was a wonderful conker ! It would smash everyone else's to bits !

And it did, too ! No other conker could stand against Lennie's. Bang ! The conker would be smashed to bits as Lennie's hit it, fair and square. Lennie had found it under this very tree ten days ago. Now everyone was hunting there again, for the wind had blown down many more, and perhaps someone would find another giant conker—one that would conquer even Lennie's fifty-three-er !

It was George who found the Very Fat Conker. He was shuffling about in the mass of prickly chestnut cases on the ground when his foot kicked an extra large case, set with

enormous prickles. It hadn't even burst open when it had struck the ground.

" Here's a jolly big case ! " said George, picking it up. " Big as an orange—look, Lennie. I bet there are big chestnuts in this ! "

He split the case, and there, lying snugly in a white woolly bed, were three conkers—one tiny one, not much bigger than a pea, one small one the size of a hazel nut—and one GIANT of a conker, big and fat and sturdy !

" Oh I say—look what George has got ! " said Lennie. "George, I'll swop my new pencil for that conker."

" No, thanks," said George. " I'm keeping it myself. I'll fight your fifty-three-er with it, Lennie. It will smash it like an egg-shell."

" It won't," said Lennie, though he secretly thought that it might. " Go on—take my new pencil—and I'll give you a rubber too, if you like. I bet my fifty three-er would smash it, and then it will be gone. I'd just like to keep it for a second fighting-conker, in case my fifty-three-er gets cracked or smashed."

"No," said George, firmly. "I'm going to keep this conker for myself and fight yours with it."

And he did keep it, no matter how Lennie followed him about, offering him this and that for it. Then came the day when George challenged Lennie to fight with his conker against the Giant, as everyone called George's fat chestnut.

George had bored a hole through it very carefully. He had taken some strong string, threaded it through, and knotted it well. He had tried out his conker against several smaller ones and had conquered them all.

Hilda had held out her conker for George's to hit—and the Giant had smashed it to bits. John had held out his

elevener, a sturdy little conker that had already broken eleven others—and this had been broken in half. Then Fred challenged George with his, a fine big one but not very solid.

" Go on, hit it," said Fred. " I bet it will be strong enough to resist yours ! " It was—but alas, when Fred hit George's conker in his turn he hadn't broken George's—his own had cracked all the way round instead, so that was the end of it.

And now George had challenged Lennie's great conker, the king of them all. The whole class, both boys and girls, gathered round to watch. They were in the playground of the school, down by the shrubbery, and they all watched the battle eagerly.

George held his conker up first, dangling on its string, so that Lennie could strike it with his great conker. Lennie took a careful look at it, and then swung his and brought it down hard on George's conker. Crash ! Everyone blinked, expecting George's to fly into pieces. But it didn't. No, it swung backwards and forwards without a mark on it. It was certainly a wonderful conker !

" Now my turn ! " said George. " Hold yours out, Lennie, while I think exactly where to hit it."

Lennie held it out, and it twisted a little at the end of its string. Then George swung his—and hit Lennie's with such a mighty blow that it flew into a hundred pieces and spattered everyone with tiny bits of brown skin and white nut.

" He's conquered Lennie's ! " cried Fred. " What is your conker now, George ? "

" A hundred-and-fiver," said George proudly. " Sorry to smash such a good conker as yours, Lennie, but . . ." Lennie stared at his bit of string, with just a tiny bit of conker left beside the knot. He was not a good loser, and he just *couldn't* say, " Jolly good, George. The best conker wins ! " as most people said. His face went red, and he felt very very angry. He

suddenly caught hold of George's conker and snatched it away from him, string and all. He flung it violently into the air, and it went sailing away into the shrubbery.

"There! I hope it's lost for ever!" he said, and ran off at top speed, leaving everyone most amazed.

" Good gracious—what a temper!" said Hilda, shocked.

" Oh, George—quick, let's go and find your conker."

They all ran to look until the bell went for the end of break. But nobody found it—and that wasn't surprising because the

string had caught on the branch of a laurel bush, and the conker hung down in the middle of the green leaves, quite hidden.

George was very upset.

" My hundred and-fiver ! " he said. " I'll never see it again. How disgusting of Lennie to behave like that ! "

But George did see his conker again. He found it two years later, when he was helping to tidy up the school shrubbery which had grown far too thick. The conker had fallen from the laurel bush to the damp ground, still wearing its long tail of string.

There it had put out a root, and then a shoot—and had grown into a tiny tree, and when George suddenly saw the fine little chestnut tree it was about two feet high and had three or four sets of fan-shaped leaves !

" I say—come and look—this must be the big fat conker I

lost!" shouted George in delight. "Look, it's still got its string! My word—I do hope the Head will let it stay here!"

He did, because he was so interested in the tale of the Very Fat Conker when George told it to him. And now the little tree is eighteen years old, and a lovely one too—tall and green and shady.

Each autumn it throws down big fat conkers in prickly cases —and all the children, remembering the tale of the hundred-and fiver-er, go hunting to find one just as good. And one day someone will!

The Clever Gnome

"How shall I cross this bubbling stream?"
Wondered the little gnome.
"It's much too deep for paddling through,
But I really *must* get home.
I know what I'll do—here's a toadstool brown,
I'll pick it—and turn it so—
And launch it like this on the running stream
And then like a boat it will go!
A leaf for a paddle, and now I'm off
In my dear little toadstool ship.
Good-bye, good-bye—I shall soon be home,
And I *am* enjoying my trip!"

Tommy's White Duck

TOMMY had a real live duck of his own. He had had it given to him when it was just a little yellow duckling, and somehow or other nobody had ever thought what it would be like when it grew up!

At first it was just a dear little yellow bird, crying " Peep, peep, peep! " all day. Daddy made it a tiny run of its own, with wire netting all round, and a small coop for it to sleep in. Tommy fed it and gave it a small bowl of water to swim in.

And then, quite suddenly, it seemed, it began to grow! By the time the middle of the summer came it was quite a big duck. It had lost its pretty yellow down and grew snowy-white feathers. It no longer said " Peep, peep! " but " Quack, quack, quack! " in quite a loud voice.

Daddy had to make the run bigger. The days went on, and the duck grew and grew. It could no longer swim in the bowl, nor even in the tin bath Mummy put for it.

" Daddy, could we make a little pond for my duck? " asked Tommy one day. " I could help you to dig it out, couldn't I? "

" Dear me, I'm not going to dig a pond for that noisy old duck! " said Daddy. " It's got too big for us now, Tommy. We shall have to sell it."

" Daddy! " cried Tommy, his eyes full of tears. " Sell my duck! Oh, I couldn't! Why, perhaps somebody would have it for their dinner—it would be simply dreadful! "

" Well, dear, it's really too big now," said Daddy. " Besides, it has such a noisy quack."

"But, Daddy, if we made it a little pond of its own, it would be happy and wouldn't quack for one," said Tommy. "I'm sure that's why it's quacking such a lot—because it wants a swim."

"Well, Tommy, what about letting the farmer's wife have the duck back?" asked Daddy. "She gave it to you when it was a duckling, and maybe she'd like it back now, to go with her other ducks. Then it could swim on her big pond."

Tommy didn't say any more. He could see that Daddy didn't want the duck, and that it would have to go. But he was very sad about it, and he went slowly out to the garden to talk to the duck.

"Quack!" said the duck joyfully when it saw Tommy.

"Hallo," said Tommy. "Dear old duck, I'm afraid you're going to be given away, and won't live with me any more."

" Quack ! " said the duck, and gave Tommy a small, loving peck.

Well, the very next day the duck was taken down the lane to the farm, and Tommy had to say good-bye to it. The duck seemed very puzzled, but when it saw the other ducks it went quite mad with joy and dashed into the pond, waddling so fast that it fell over its own big flat feet ! "

" There you are ! " said Daddy, turning to Tommy. " See how pleased the duck is to be here ! "

" But it will miss me when it's got used to being here," said Tommy. " It will want me, Daddy."

" Nonsense ! " said Daddy, laughing, and he took Tommy home.

Well, it so happened that Tommy was right, for the very next day the duck had a look round and thought, " Where's

Tommy ? Where's my own run ? Where's the garden I know so well ? Where, oh where, is Tommy ? "

The duck sat in the sun and thought. It loved Tommy and wanted to be with him. So what did it do but walk over the farmyard and squeeze under the gate, and set off waddling up the lane, back to Tommy's house and garden !

" Quack ! " it said as it went. " Quack ! " Up the dusty lane it went, and at last it came to Tommy's house. Nobody was in. Tommy was at school. Tommy's daddy was at work. Tommy's mother had slipped in the house next door to talk to Mrs. White. But the baby was in her pram in the garden fast asleep.

" Quack ! " said the duck, squeezing through the hedge and looking round for Tommy. But just then something happened. There came the sound of thundering hoofs and two of the farm-horses galloped up the lane !

Someone had left the field-gate open, and the horses had got out. They were excited and were running after one another. And what do you think happened ? Why, one of them saw the garden-gate open and galloped through into the garden !

The duck knew quite well this was wrong. Suppose the horse knocked the pram over? Good gracious, look at the mess it was making of the lovely lawn, sinking its hard heels deep into the grass!

There was only one thing to do, and the duck knew what it was! It knew quite well that usually when it quacked loudly, Tommy's mother came to the window and said, "Sh! Sh! You'll wake the baby!" And if only the duck could make her come, she would see the galloping horse and everything would be put right! The duck didn't know that Tommy's mother was not in the house, of course.

It began to quack. How it quacked! You should have heard it! "Quack, quack, quack, quack, QUACK, QUACK, QUACK!"

Tommy's mother heard the loud quacking from the next-door house. "Well!" she said in surprise, "that sounds just like our duck—but it can't be, because Daddy took it down to the farm yesterday."

"Quack, quack, quack, quack, QUACK, QUACK!" cried the duck, as the horse galloped round the garden once more.

"It *must* be our duck!" said Tommy's mother and she ran back home to see—and, of course, she at once saw the horse in the garden!

"Oh! Oh!" she cried. "It will knock the pram over! It will knock the pram over!"

She caught up a stick and ran to the excited horse. She drove it to the gate—and it went out at a gallop, off down the lane to the farm, where the other horse had also gone.

Mummy shut the gate. She was quite pale and frightened. Tommy came running home from school and wondered what was the matter.

"Oh, Tommy!" said Mummy, "one of those great farm-

horses got into the garden this afternoon when I was next door, and nearly knocked the pram over!"

"But how did you know it was here, galloping about?" asked Tommy. "Did you hear Baby crying?"

"No—I heard your old duck quacking!" said Mummy. "Fancy that, Tommy! It must have walked all the way up the lane to get back to *you*—and it quacked loudly when it saw the horse, and warned me."

"Oh, you good old duck!" cried Tommy, running to his duck and putting his arms round its snowy neck. "You good old thing! You saved Baby! Mummy—I do wish we could keep my duck! Look how it's come all the way home again!"

"You *shall* keep it," said Mummy, and she patted the surprised duck on the head. "When I tell Daddy about how it warned me this afternoon by quacking so loudly, he will be sure to say it can stay with you now."

So Mummy told Daddy—and what do you think he and Tommy are doing this week ? Guess !

Yes—they are both digging out a nice little pond for the duck, for it is to stay with Tommy, of course. Won't it be pleased to have a pond of its own ! Yesterday it laid its first egg—and Daddy had it for breakfast !

" Quack ! " said the duck. " I'm one of the family. You can't get rid of me ! Quack ! "

The New Doll

Who do you suppose is in
My dolly's cot to-day?
Come and pull the cover back
Just a little way.

Yes, it's Pussy lying there,
A night-cap on her head,
I put her in and tucked her up,
She loves her cosy bed!

But Dolly's rather cross—she sulks—
And when I've gone to play
I'm sure she'll turn my pussy out
And send her right away!

The Mischievous Tunnel

JIMMY had a railway train that ran by clockwork on toy railway-lines. He had a little station too, with porters and passengers standing on it. He had a fine signal that went up and down—and he had a tunnel for the train to go under.

But that tunnel was too mischievous for anything! It always managed to set itself just a bit crooked when the train came rushing through—and, of course, the engine knocked into it, ran off the lines, and fell over. Then Jimmy would shout loudly :

" An accident ! An accident ! "

The tunnel thought this was great fun. It didn't matter how carefully Jimmy set the tunnel over the lines, it always managed to make itself crooked when the train came running by. And always there was an accident.

At first Jimmy and Jane, his sister, thought this was rather fun. But when it happened every time they got tired of it.

"I wish the train would run round and round properly until the clockwork was run down," said Jimmy. "It always falls off by the tunnel."

"Well, it shouldn't," said Jane, looking through the tunnel. "The tunnel doesn't touch the lines, Jimmy. It's supposed to be quite wide enough for the train to run through. I think it's a mischievous tunnel. Look—I've set it so that the train can run right through without touching at all."

"All right," said Jimmy. "I'll put lots of passengers on the train, Jane, and give them a good trip. And I'll put some

toy cows into the cow-trucks too. The guard shall go in the guard's van. My, it's a full train. It mustn't have an accident *this* time ! "

Well, when the tunnel heard what a lot of passengers were going to be on the train, it felt more mischievous than ever. It would certainly upset the train if it could—and then what a lot of people would fall out !

So once again it set itself just a bit crooked so that it touched the line.

Jimmy wound up the engine. The signal looked at the crooked tunnel and spoke to it.

" Tunnel ! I can see you've put yourself crooked. Now don't play tricks this time. You know quite well that Jimmy and Jane are tired of them. Don't upset the train."

" I shall do as I like," said the tunnel, and set itself more crooked than ever.

Jimmy set the engine down on the line. He hooked the

coal-truck on to it. Behind were all the carriages, the cow-trucks, and the guard's van.

It was a fine long train, but the engine was strong and could quite well pull them all.

Jimmy waved his green flag. The signal worked. Jane whistled. The train was off.

Round the lines it sped, as fast as it could, and behind it ran all the trucks as happy as could be, with the dolls jerking up and down in them, and the cows looking out of their trucks too.

The engine reached the tunnel. Its key caught against it. It ran off the lines. The carriages all fell over. Out tumbled the dolls and the cows. Another accident—and a bad one this time!

"Oh dear! This little doll has broken her arm!" said Jane. "And this cow has broken off her tail. Bother that horrid tunnel. We won't use it for a tunnel any more!"

Jane picked up the tunnel and put it away from the lines.

"But what else can a tunnel be used for?" Jimmy asked.

"I'll soon show you!" said Jane, and she went to the doll's chest. She took out a little mattress, a pillow, a bolster, two sheets, and two blankets. She turned the tunnel upside down, and neatly arranged all the bedclothes inside.

"It shall be a cradle for my baby-doll!" she said. "I haven't a bed small enough for her—and the tunnel will do nicely. If it can't behave like a proper tunnel, it shall behave like a cradle!"

Well, you should have heard the signal and the porters, the passengers and the engine driver laugh when they saw what was happening to the tunnel. A baby-doll's cradle! Well, well, well!

As for the tunnel, it was in a great rage; but it couldn't turn itself the right way up—so there it is still, a nice little cradle for the baby-doll. And doesn't it wish it was a proper tunnel again, watching the railway train rush round and round and round! Maybe if Jimmy ever gives it another chance it will really try to behave itself.

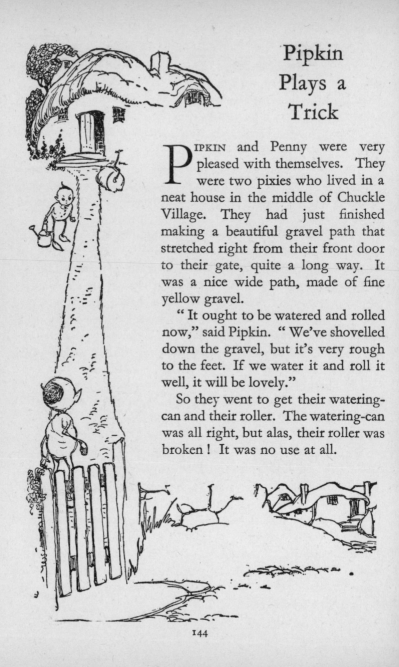

Pipkin
Plays a
Trick

Pipkin and Penny were very pleased with themselves. They were two pixies who lived in a neat house in the middle of Chuckle Village. They had just finished making a beautiful gravel path that stretched right from their front door to their gate, quite a long way. It was a nice wide path, made of fine yellow gravel.

"It ought to be watered and rolled now," said Pipkin. "We've shovelled down the gravel, but it's very rough to the feet. If we water it and roll it well, it will be lovely."

So they went to get their watering-can and their roller. The watering-can was all right, but alas, their roller was broken! It was no use at all.

" We must borrow one," said Penny. " Mister Grip has a nice one. Let's go and ask him to lend it to us."

So they went to Mister Grip's house—but he was a surly fellow, and wouldn't lend it.

" No," he said, " I don't lend things to pixies. They are too careless."

" We're *not* careless ! " said Pipkin, quite cross. " We always look after things that are lent to us and take them back again."

But Mister Grip banged his door in their faces and the two pixies had to go.

" We'll ask Dame Roundy if she'll lend us *her* roller," said Penny, hopefully. " Hers is a fine big one."

So off they went to Dame Roundy's. She was making cakes and said she couldn't be bothered to get the key of her garden shed.

" Go and ask someone else," she said, impatiently. " I can't trouble about it now."

Pipkin and Penny went away. They thought it was very un-kind of Dame Roundy.

" We'll go to the gnome Chiffle-Chuffle," said Pipkin. " His roller is very big indeed."

They knocked at the door of Chiffle-Chuffle's house. There was no answer. But Pipkin suddenly saw the gnome's face peeping through the window at them, and he called him.

" Chiffle-Chuffle, answer the door! We've come to ask you to lend us your big roller."

The gnome slipped his head inside and made no answer. He was pretending not to be in. He didn't want to lend his roller to the pixies.

Pipkin and Penny knocked as loudly as they could once more, for they knew quite well that Chiffle-Chuffle was at home—but it was no good, he wouldn't open the door. So off they went down the garden-path, very angry with Chiffle-Chuffle for being so mean.

" There's only Mrs. Tippitty left who's got a roller," said Penny. " Oh, I do hope she will lend it to us. She's such a cross old thing that I'm afraid she won't."

He was quite right. Mrs. Tippitty was in a very bad temper that afternoon, and when she heard that the pixies wanted to borrow her roller she went quite purple with rage.

" What, lend my fine roller to two careless pixies like you ! " she cried. " Whatever next ? No, indeed—and run away quickly before I box your ears ! "

You should have seen Pipkin and Penny run ! They knew quite well that Mrs. Tippitty meant what she said, for she had often boxed their ears before. They went home and looked sadly at their gravel path. It did so badly want rolling.

And then Pipkin had a great idea. He whispered it to Penny, who was simply delighted.

" When Mister Grip, Dame Roundy, Chiffle-Chuffle and Mrs. Tippitty come by our cottage to-day on their way back from their shopping we will play your trick on them," said Penny. " It's a clever plan ! "

What do you think it was ? Ah, you wait and see !

After tea Mister Grip, Dame Roundy, Chiffle-Chuffle and Mrs. Tippitty all passed by to do their shopping in Chuckle Village. Pipkin and Penny watched them from their window.

" In about half-an-hour they'll be back again," said Pipkin, excited. " Go out and hide that farthing of yours down deep in the gravel, Penny."

Penny slipped out and dug a little hole in the new gravel path. He hid a farthing there and then carefully covered it up. Then he and Pipkin waited for the shoppers to return. Chiffle-Chuffle came first, carrying a big bag of potatoes.

As soon as the pixies saw him they pretended to be very busy

hunting for something in the gravel path. He stopped to ask them if they had lost something.

"There's some money somewhere in the gravel," said Pipkin.

"I'll help you to look for it," said Chiffle-Chuffle, hoping that if he found it the two pixies would give him some of it for his trouble. So in at the gate he came and began to walk up and down the new gravel path looking for the money. He had enormous feet, and how they crunched the gravel as he walked.

Then Dame Roundy, as plump as her name, and with big goloshes on her feet, peeped over the gate, looking in surprise at the two pixies and the gnome hunting up and down the path.

"What are you looking for?" she asked.

"Money," said the gnome Chiffle-Chuffle. "We don't need your help. Go away."

Well, of course, Dame Roundy wasn't going to be ordered away by Chiffle-Chuffle like that! No, she got very red and glared at the gnome in a rage.

" Oh, you want to find the money and keep it for yourself, do you, Chiffle-Chuffle ! " she said. " Well, I'll just come in and look too, to see fair play ! "

To the pixies' great delight in she came and began to plod up and down the gravel path with her heavy goloshes, looking and looking for the money.

" She's better than a roller ! " whispered Pipkin to Penny. " Her goloshes squash the gravel down beautifully ! "

Soon along came Mister Grip and Mrs. Tippitty, walking together. They stopped in surprise when they saw so many people walking up and down the pixies' gravel path.

" Come and help too ! " cried Dame Roundy. " We are looking for some money ! "

In went Mister Grip and Mrs. Tippitty, eager to join the fun. Mrs. Tippitty had small feet so she really wasn't much use to press down the gravel, but Mister Grip had his great Wellington boots on, and they were fine for the gravel.

Well, you should have seen them all hunting up and down that gravel path, looking for the money. They didn't know it was only a farthing, they just hunted and hunted. And the

gravel path got smoother and smoother and smoother, just as if it had been carefully rolled by their rollers ! It was fine to see it, and the two pixies couldn't help chuckling.

At last when the path was as smooth as could be, Pipkin and Penny thought it was time for everyone to go.

" Never mind about looking any more," said Penny. " Thank you all very much. You haven't found the money, but you've made our path nice and smooth for us."

Then Mister Grip, Dame Roundy, Chiffle-Chuffle and Mrs. Tippitty all suddenly remembered that the pixies had asked to borrow their rollers that day—and they looked at the path and saw how their feet had flattened it out nicely, almost as well as a roller would have done. Then they knew that a trick had been played on them and they were angry.

" It's a trick ! " cried Mrs. Tippitty.

" There isn't any money in the path ! " roared Chiffle-Chuffle.

" It's because we wouldn't lend the pixies our rollers ! " shouted Mister Grip.

" I'll smack them ! " said Dame Roundy. But the pixies were too quick for her. They ran into their house and banged the door. Pipkin opened the window and leaned out.

" There *is* some money in the gravel ! " he cried. " There really is."

" Well, you tell us where it is, or we'll punish you," said Mister Grip, shaking his fist.

" Yes, and we'll keep the money too, for our trouble in looking for it ! " cried Dame Roundy.

" Well, if we tell you where it is and let you share it between you, will you go away quietly and not worry us any more ? " said Penny.

" Yes ! " shouted everyone.

" Do you see that red snapdragon leaning over the path just

there ? " said Penny. " Well, dig up the path a little by it and you'll find the money."

Mister Grip did as Penny said ; and very soon he found the farthing. He picked it up and looked at it. When he saw it was only a farthing he was so angry that he flung it straight at the two grinning pixies, who had their heads out of the window to see what was happening.

The others, who hadn't seen that it was only a farthing, were angry with Mister Grip for throwing the money to Pipkin and Penny. They ran at him and if he hadn't slipped out of the gate very quickly indeed he would have had his coat pulled right off ! He tore down the lane and Dame Roundy, Chiffle-Chuffle and Mrs. Tippitty raced after him.

Pipkin and Penny leaned against one another and laughed till they cried. Then they picked up the farthing from the floor and put it into their money-box.

" That will teach Dame Roundy and the others not to be so mean about lending things another time," said Penny, looking out on his nice smooth gravel path.

" Yes, it will," said Pipkin, rubbing his hands together in delight. " They've wasted lots of time in looking for a farthing which they didn't get in the end—and they've flattened out our new path for us nicely ! Ha ha, ho ho ! "

You should see the path. It's the best in Chuckle Village !

The Runaway Hen

"I'M just going to take Diana Susan for a ride in her pram, Mummy!" called Betty. "I won't be long. I'm only going down to the end of the lane and back again."

"Well, post this letter for me, darling," said Mummy, and Betty took it and slipped it under Diana Susan's pillow. Then off she went, out of the gate and down the lane.

She heard the cluck-luck-lucking of Mrs. Dawkins' hens next door, and wondered if one of them had laid an egg. What a lot of cackling was going on ! She peeped through the hedge to see why.

Goodness—there was a dog chasing the hens—and one hen was racing up the garden as fast as she could go, with the dog after her. It was only a puppy, and meant to have a game, but the hen didn't know that ! It fled out of the gate and ran down the lane.

" Puppy ! Stop that ! " shouted Betty. " What's your name now ? I've forgotten. Oh yes—Tinker. Come here, Tinker. It's very very bad to chase hens. You'll get into trouble if you do things like that. Go home ! " And she pointed sternly down the road.

Tinker put his tail down and ran off at once. He knew quite well he had done wrong. " It's all right, hens, he's gone ! " Betty called through the hedge. Then she remembered the hen that had run down the lane. Had she better tell Mrs. Dawkins about it ? No, perhaps she had better see if she could find the hen. So down the lane she went, wheeling Diana Susan in her lovely blue pram, keeping her eyes open for the hen.

She couldn't see it anywhere. Whatever could have hap-

pened to it? Then she saw it, still running fast, going towards the main road. Betty called to it.

"Hen! Don't go there! There are cars whizzing along at sixty miles an hour! Come back, hen!"

But the hen took no notice at all. It was quite lost, it was afraid that the puppy was still chasing it, and it meant to run and run and run!

"Oh, you silly little hen," said Betty, pushing her pram as fast as she could. "If only you'd come back this way I could get behind you and shoo you home."

The hen still ran on and on, and at last came to the main road. A car whizzed by so quickly that the poor hen had quite a shock. She thought it must be a very big puppy. Then another car came by, saw the hen and hooted.

The hen scuttled into the hedge. Yes, that must have been another puppy, because it said "parp-parp", and sounded very like the puppy's barking. The hen peered out of the hedge, wondering if it could make a dash for the other side of the road. Perhaps it would find the other hens there. It really didn't know where it was at all!

Just as Betty came up to where the lane met the main road the hen made a dash across it. A car whizzed by at the same moment, just avoiding the hen, but frightening it very much indeed. It sank down at the side of the road and drooped its head on to its chest. Betty left her pram and hurried over to the hen.

" Are you hurt ? " she said. " Or just very frightened ? Oh, you poor creature, you do look ill! Can you walk ? If you can, I'll guide you home."

But the hen couldn't walk. It had had such a scare that it couldn't even stand. It just lay there, looking very feathery and floppy, its eyes half closed.

" I'll carry you safely across, back to my pram," said Betty, and picked up the hen in her arms. It felt quite heavy. It gave a feeble cluck and then lay quite still. Betty carried it over the road to her pram.

" I don't know what to do with you," she said. " You can't walk. And I can't carry you all the way home and wheel my pram too. Well—I hope my doll won't mind, but I'm afraid you'll have to ride in the pram too, hen ! "

Betty moved her doll to one side and put the hen into the pram. It didn't seem to mind at all. It gave another little cluck

F

and then settled down in a big feathery heap. The doll looked surprised, but she didn't seem to mind either.

" Now I'll wheel you home, so please be sensible and don't fly out of the pram," said Betty, and she began to push the pram slowly back down the lane.

The hen shut its eyes and seemed to go to sleep. A man came hurrying by on his way to catch the bus and he was MOST astonished to see a hen in the doll's pram. He simply couldn't understand it, but he didn't say anything about it because he was already late for the bus.

When Betty came near to her own front gate she saw her mother there talking to Mrs. Dawkins, who had just come back from doing her shopping in the village.

" Oh, there you are, Betty," said Mummy. " Have you had a—why . . . good gracious me ! WHATEVER have you got in your pram ? "

" A hen ! " said Mrs. Dawkins. " And it looks like one of mine. Well I never ! Do you usually take my hens for rides in your pram, Betty ? "

" Oh no. But a puppy chased the hens," explained Betty.

" And this one was frightened and ran down the lane to the main road. A car nearly ran over it and it felt ill, so I put it into my pram to bring it back home. I do hope it isn't hurt."

Mrs. Dawkins lifted it out and looked at it carefully. It suddenly opened its wings and flung itself out of Mrs. Dawkins' arms. It ran down the road, squawking loudly, and scuttled in to join the others. " Not much wrong with it,"

said Mrs. Dawkins, laughing. " Well, you *are* kind, Betty, to bring my hen home."

" Did you post my letter, dear ? " asked Mummy.

" Oh dear—no ! " said Betty. " The hen made me forget." She groped under the doll's pillow for the letter, and then gave a squeal of surprise. " Here's the letter—and something else as well. Oh LOOK ! " And she brought out a big brown egg and the letter too. How Mummy and Mrs. Dawkins laughed.

" Well ! It wanted to give you a present for helping it," said Mrs. Dawkins. " You must have that for your breakfast. I'm sure it will taste very good ! "

It did, and Betty enjoyed it very much. It was nice of the hen, wasn't it ? It sometimes lays an egg under the hedge between Mrs. Dawkins' garden and Betty's, and then Mrs. Dawkins says Betty must have it, because she is sure that the hen means it for her. I expect she does, too !

The Good Old Rocking-Horse

IN the nursery there was a big old rocking-horse. His name was Dobbin, and he was on rockers that went to and fro, to and fro, when anyone rode on him.

He was a dear old horse, and it was very queer that the toys didn't like him! They were afraid of him—and it was all because of something that was quite an accident.

It happened like this. One day the toy monkey fell off the shelf nearby, and went bump on to the floor. His long tail spread itself out, and a bit of it went under one of the rocking-horse's rockers.

Well, that didn't matter a bit—until John got up on to the horse and rocked to and fro. Then, of course, the rocking-horse pinched the monkey's tail hard every time he rocked over it, and the monkey sobbed and cried after John had gone to bed.

"You great big, unkind thing!" sobbed the poor monkey, holding his tail between his paws. "You nearly squashed my tail in half. You hurt me dreadfully. I nearly squealed out loud when John was riding you. I don't like you one bit."

"Listen, monkey," said the rocking-horse in his deep,

gentle voice, " I didn't mean to do that. I didn't even know that your tail was there. And in any case I couldn't help it, because John rocked me so hard. But do believe me when I say that I am very, very sorry. I wouldn't have hurt you for the world ! "

" I should just think you *are* sorry ! " wept the monkey. " Oh my poor tail ! Whatever shall I do with it ? "

The golliwog came up with a bandage. The baby-doll came up with a bowl of water. They bathed the tail and then bound up the squashed end with the bandage. The monkey looked at his tail and felt rather grand when he saw how important it looked with a bandage round it.

It was quite better after a time—but somehow the toys really never forgave the rocking-horse, and he was very sad about it. He knew that he couldn't have helped rocking over the monkey's tail—it was really John's fault for leaving his monkey on the floor—but the toys never seemed to understand that.

So they didn't ask Dobbin to play games with them, and they never even said " yes" when he asked them to have a ride on his back. They just shook their heads and said " no." This hurt the rocking-horse very much, because there was nothing he liked better than giving people rides.

" They think I'm unkind, though I'm not," he thought sadly. " Well—I suppose they will always think the same and I must just put up with it."

Helen Jacobs

Now the toys were very friendly with a little red squirrel who lived in the pine-trees at the bottom of the garden. He often used to come leaping up to the window-sill to talk to them. Sometimes he even came right into the nursery, and he was delighted one day when they got out one of the dolls' hair-brushes and brushed his beautiful bushy tail for him.

"Oh, thank you," he said. "Thank you very much indeed. That's so kind of you. I'll bring you a present one day, Toys."

Helen Jacobs

So when the autumn came he brought them a present. It was two pawfuls of nuts! He had picked them from the hazel trees for the toys.

"Here you are," he said. "Nuts for you. They are most delicious! You must crack the hard shell and inside you will find a lovely white nut. I do hope you will like them. Good-bye!"

He sprang off to find some nuts for himself. He meant to hide some in cracks and corners, so that if he awoke in the cold winter days he might find his nuts and have a meal.

The toys looked at the nuts. They were so excited and pleased because they didn't often get any presents. They longed to eat the nuts and see what they tasted like.

The golly put one into his mouth and tried to crack the shell.

But he couldn't. It was much too hard. Then the brown toy dog tried to crack one. But even he couldn't! Then the toys threw the nuts hard on to the floor, but not one cracked.

"We shan't be able to eat the nuts," said the brown dog sadly. "They will be wasted!"

"Let us get the little hammer out of the toy tool-box," said the bear. "Perhaps we can break the nuts with that."

So they looked for the toy hammer and they found it. They put a nut on the floor and hit hard with the hammer. But the nut jumped away each time, unbroken. It was most tiresome.

Then the rocking-horse spoke up in his deep, gentle voice. "I can crack your nuts for you, Toys! If you will put them underneath my rockers I can rock over them and crack the shells! One of you must ride me to and fro, and then I can easily crack the nuts for you."

The toys all looked at one another. They badly wanted their nuts cracked, so they thought they would do as Dobbin said. They laid all the nuts in a row under his rockers. Then the golliwog climbed up on the horse's back and began to rock him to and fro.

Crick-crack, crick-crack went all the nuts as the shells broke. Inside were the lovely white kernels, so sweet and delicious to eat !

Helen Jacobs

" Thank you, Dobbin ! " said the toys. The golliwog patted him and slid down to get his nuts.

" That was a lovely ride I had ! " he whispered to the other toys. " I wouldn't mind another ! "

" Have as many as you like ! " said Dobbin, who heard what the golly said. " Are the nuts nice ? "

" Delicious ! Have one ? " said the bear, and he held one up for Dobbin to nibble. " It was kind of you to crack them for us—very friendly indeed."

" I'm such a friendly person," said the rocking-horse sadly, " but you won't make friends with me. I would so much like to give you all a ride."

He looked so sad that the monkey suddenly felt very sorry for him. In a trice he had leapt up on to Dobbin's back.

" Gee-up ! " he cried. " I'll be friends with you ! Gee-up ! "

And then, one after another, all the toys had a ride, and after that they were as friendly as could be. Wasn't it a good thing Dobbin offered to crack their nuts for them ?

Joan's Nice Big Coconut

JOHNNY was ill in bed, and the little girl next door was sorry for him. " What's the matter with Johnny, Mummy ? " she said. " Can't he come to the Fair with me this afternoon ? You said you'd take us both."

" No, he can't, Joan dear," said her mother. " He has something wrong with his tummy, and he must stay in bed for a week or two till it's better."

So Joan and Mummy had to go to the Fair without Johnny. Joan went for a ride on the roundabout, but it wasn't much fun by herself. She went for a swing on the swing-boats with another girl whom she didn't know—but the girl made the swing go too high and Joan didn't like it.

" I'm not enjoying myself very much," she said to her mother. " I wish Johnny was here. Oh look—what are all those coconuts for, sitting up in little cups over there ? "

" That's a coconut shy," said Mummy. " You buy three wooden balls for sixpence, and you throw them at the coconuts—and if you knock one down, you have it for yourself."

" What—to take *home* ? " said Joan. " And eat ? "

" Yes, to take home—but you won't want to eat much of it," said Mummy. " A coconut is so big ! Look, here is a sixpence, Joan. See if you can knock down a coconut ! "

Joan was pleased. She gave her sixpence to the man at the coconut shy, and he gave her three round wooden balls. She threw the first one—and dear me, it didn't go anywhere *near* a coconut ! Then she threw her second one, much more carefully, but that didn't hit a coconut either.

"I'm no good at this!" said Joan, and flung her last wooden ball as hard as she could at a big fat coconut at the back.

Bumpity-bump! It knocked against the big nut and bumped it right off its wooden cup. "Ooooh! Can I have it?" said Joan, pleased. The man gave it to her and she ran to her mother.

"Mummy! I knocked off a coconut, the biggest of them all!" she said proudly. "And do you know what I'm going to do with it? I'm going to give it to Johnny because he's ill and couldn't come to the Fair!"

"Well, he won't be allowed to eat it, dear," said Mummy. "So I'm afraid it will be wasted."

"He might be allowed just a very *tiny* bit," said Joan, and hugged the big coconut under her arm till she had to go home. She went in to see Johnny straight away. "Johnny!" she said, as soon as she was in his bedroom. "Look what I got at the Fair—the very biggest coconut of all, and it's for *you*! "

" Ooooh—I do like coconut," said Johnny. " I'll ask Mummy to break it and we'll eat some. Oh, here she is ! Mummy, look what Joan's brought—a coconut that she won at the Fair. It's for me ! Will you break it, please, and give me a piece. I do like coconut ! "

" Oh, darling, no," said his mother. " You can't possibly eat coconut with such a bad tummy. It would make you feel very ill indeed."

" It wouldn't," said Johnny. " It would make me feel better. I can't waste it, Mummy. PLEASE let me have a piece. Daddy doesn't like coconut, nor do you, nor does Granny. Nobody does but me ! "

" I know somebody who likes it very much," said his mother, smiling. " It won't be wasted. I know quite a number of little guests who would be glad to come and have some here."

" Who ? " said Johnny and Joan at once.

" You'll see," said Johnny's mother, and she went out of the room with the coconut. Soon she was back, and Johnny saw that she had split it into two halves. Inside the rough shell was the snowy-white nut. Johnny longed to have a piece.

" No, dear, you can't," said Mummy. " But Joan can have some if she likes."

" Not if Johnny can't, thank you, Mrs. Haines," said Joan. " What are you going to do with it now ? Who likes it ? "

" You wait and see ! " said Mummy, and she went to the window and opened it. Johnny saw that she had a nail in her hand, and a hammer, and a piece of string. He and Joan watched carefully as she hammered the nail into the wood at the side of the window, then tied one half of the coconut with the string and hung it on the nail. Then she hung the other half just below it.

"Now you and Joan watch the nut while you are playing cards," she said. "And you're sure to see a little visitor—perhaps two or three!"

Well, Johnny's mother was right! In about ten minutes there was a sudden flutter of wings, and down to the nut flew a beautiful little bird dressed in blue and yellow, and with a bright blue cap. "Pim-im-im-im-im-im!" he said, and cocked a bright little eye at the children, who were watching in delight. He began to peck vigorously at the coconut. Then there came another call, and a second bird flew down—a bigger one, with more green on him, and black cap. "Pe-ter, Pe-ter, Pe-ter-Pete!" he called loudly.

Just then Mummy came into the room and saw both birds. "Why, your visitors are here already!" she said. "Look, the tiny one is a blue tit—and the big one is a great-tit. They both love coconut. You are sure to have them here every day and they will bring their families too!"

Mummy was right. The tits were on the coconut all day long and Johnny was never dull for a single minute! He felt much better, and his appetite came back so that he ate quite big meals again. The doctor was very pleased. "And what's made you feel well so quickly, I wonder?" he said. "There hasn't been much sunshine for you!"

"It's coconut that has put me right," said Johnny solemnly, and that made the doctor look at his mother in horror.

"Surely he hasn't been eating *coconut*!" he said.

"No—but my friends have!" said Johnny, and he pointed to the half-coconuts, with two blue tits pecking away and a great-tit nearby. How the doctor laughed!

"Well, well!" he said. "It's a pity all ill children can't use a coconut in that way. We really ought to tell them!"

So that's why I've told *you*! You'll know what to ask for when you're ill—a nice big coconut hanging at the side of your window!

The Boy Who Wouldn't Race

IT was such fun by the sea. Ronnie was there with his mother, and so were many other children. They had a lovely time digging and paddling and bathing.

In the morning at ten o'clock Uncle Dick came along. He wasn't really Ronnie's uncle, or anybody else's either—but all the children called him Uncle Dick.

He was great fun. He called the boys and girls round him, made them stand in rows, and gave them all kinds of exercises to do. Then they marched after him up and down the sands— and after that there were races.

The races were exciting, because Uncle Dick always gave fine prizes to the winners. Sometimes it was a chocolate ice-

cream. Sometimes it was a bag of sweets. Sometimes it was a boat or a new spade. So all the children ran to him when he came down on the beach, eager to do exactly what he told them.

All except Ronnie. He was shy. Wasn't it a pity? Of course, lots of children are shy, but if only they knew what fun they miss, they would soon hurry up and join in everything. But Ronnie simply wouldn't.

" Ronnie, you are a very silly little boy," said his mother every morning. " Why don't you go and join the other children and do those lovely exercises and run races? It would do you such a lot of good."

" I don't like things that do me good," said Ronnie.

" Oh yes, you do! " said his mother. " Ice-creams do you good, and you like those. Oranges do you good, and you like those too. It's no good saying that to me. You get up and go to Uncle Dick. Maybe you would win a race and get a chocolate ice-cream."

" I don't want to," said Ronnie. " My legs aren't quick at running. I should be last."

" How do you know if your legs are quick or slow, if you

never run races?" said his mother. "You might have very quick legs for all you know."

"Well, I don't want to run races," said Ronnie. "I want to stay here by you."

"I think you're a baby," said his mother. "You make me cross. You're growing a big boy now, and it's time you did the things the other boys do."

But it wasn't a bit of good. Ronnie wouldn't go. Even Uncle Dick couldn't make him, though he tried to.

"Come along!" he said, holding out his hand. "You're the only little fellow on the beach who doesn't run races for me. My word, I'd like to see those legs of yours twinkling along the sands. I'm sure they can run like the wind."

"They can't," said Ronnie. "I'd be last. And I'd hate that."

" Well, somebody's got to be last," said Uncle Dick, " but they're not *always* last. Sometimes they're first. Come along, now."

But Ronnie wouldn't, so after a while Uncle Dick and his mother said no more to him. But he really couldn't help wishing he wasn't so silly when he saw the winners of the races getting ice-creams and sailing-boats !

Now, one afternoon the wind got up. Goodness me, it *was* a wind ! It whipped the waves up, and made the sea so rough that the bathers didn't dare to go out very far. Each wave had a frothy top that flew into foam. It was fun to watch them.

The children's hair blew out in the wind. A big ball flew along the beach, blown by the breeze, and two children ran after it, panting. The ships on the sea sailed by swiftly, their little sails full of wind.

Uncle Dick came down on the beach to read a book. The children didn't notice him, for most of them were building a castle a little way off. Ronnie saw him and stared at him. He thought he had the nicest face in the world, all twinkly and kind.

Uncle Dick wore a straw hat with a ribbon round. The wind played with the ribbon for a while and then it thought it would have a game with the hat. So it swooped down on it, blew round Uncle Dick's neck, and then lifted the hat off his head. Into

the air it went, ever so high—and then down to the sands! Ronnie saw it.

The wind took hold of the hat again and began to roll it swiftly along the beach. Over and over it went, and over and over.

Mother saw it. She called to Ronnie. " Ronnie, go after the hat. It will roll into the sea. Quick—Uncle Dick is so kind, you can at least do that for him ! "

Ronnie jumped up. He tore after the hat. A few other children saw it too, and they raced along the beach to get it. " Go it ! " yelled Uncle Dick. " That's the way ! Run, run ! You'll save my hat yet ! "

All the children ran their hardest. " This is a race with the hat ! " shouted one of them.

Ronnie ran as hard as he could. *He* meant to get that hat. He meant to save it from going into the sea and being spoilt. He liked Uncle Dick, and he was glad to do something for him.

Ronnie caught the hat. He pounced on it just as it was going into the water. The other children rushed up.

" How fast you run ! " they cried. " You raced the hat and us too ! "

Ronnie didn't say anything. He was quite out of breath. He went slowly back to Uncle Dick with the hat.

" Many thanks ! " said Uncle Dick. " Many, many thanks. It's an old hat, but I am fond of it. My word, how you can run ! You won that race all right, didn't you ? Allow me to give you the prize ! "

And before Ronnie could say yes or no, he felt a large chocolate ice-cream being put into his hand.

" Oh—thanks very much," he said. " That's kind of you. I *shall* enjoy it ! "

And back he ran to his mother to eat it. She looked at him proudly.

" Ronnie, you did run fast," she said. " I really felt proud to see you. What a pity you won't join the others in their races each day."

Well, the next morning when Uncle Dick came down to the beach and called the children round him, Ronnie went too ! He had been thinking about things in bed, and he had found out that he was really a silly little boy !

" What's the good of being shy and not joining in any-

thing ? " he thought. " It's only because I'm afraid of not doing so well as the others. That's cowardly. Even if I don't win many times, even if I'm last, what does it matter ? I'll have some fun. But I do believe my legs *can* run fast ! "

So to his mother's great surprise the little boy ran to join the others—and when the time came for racing, how he ran ! He wasn't first, because there were bigger boys—but he certainly wasn't last. He was third !

" Jolly good ! " cried Uncle Dick. " Now here's a boat for the first one—an ice-cream for the second one—and what about a bag of sweets for the third one ! Good for you, Ronnie ! I'm glad my hat taught you that your legs can run as fast as anybody else's ! "

It really was funny that Ronnie had to be taught a lesson by a fly-away hat, wasn't it !

What Happened to Frisky

IT was a very wet day. The twins wanted to go and play in the garden.

"Well, you may," said Mother. "But I don't want mud brought in all over the place. Wipe your feet each time you come in. If I find mud everywhere when I come back from my shopping, you'll both go to bed!"

The twins were as good as gold. They wiped their feet well on the mat and didn't leave a single muddy mark.

But Frisky the dog did. He went and walked in all the mud

he could find and then he walked indoors and left trails of dirty marks everywhere. He even got up on the couch and made the cushions muddy.

" Look at that ! " said Dan, crossly. " Frisky, you are a very very bad dog. Why don't you wipe your feet ? "

" He ought to be sent to bed," said Daisy.

" Oooh yes," said Dan. " Of course he ought. I don't see why he shouldn't have the same punishment as we should, if we'd left dirty marks all over the place."

" Frisky, come here," said Daisy. Frisky came, wagging his tail.

The children took him up to their room. " He shall go into your bed, because you thought of it," said Dan. So they lifted Frisky up, turned back the covers and pushed him down into the bed. He didn't like it at all.

" Now don't be tiresome ! " said Daisy. " You've been a bad dog and you've got to spend the day in bed. Keep still."

But Frisky struggled and barked and whined. Then Mother came in, wondering what the noise was about. How she stared when she saw the dog in Daisy's bed.

" Frisky made muddy marks downstairs," said Daisy. " So we've sent him to bed. Wasn't it a good idea, Mother ? "

But oh dear, Mother didn't think so at all ! " Just look at the way he's dirtied the clean sheets ! " she cried. " And he's torn the blanket ! Get out, Frisky, get out ! And you two can go to bed instead. What tiresome twins you are ! "